THE GOLDSMITH'S DAUGHTER

Tanya Landman is the author of many books for children. *The Goldsmith's Daughter* is her second novel for teenagers, following *Apache*.

Of *The Goldsmith's Daughter*, Tanya says, "I was intrigued by a society that was so cultured and yet so cruel – where the letting of blood was vital to nourish the sun. How did it feel to live in perpetual fear of the sun failing to rise? To have your destiny decided by the priests at the moment of your birth? If you were born under an ill-starred sky would you accept your fate meekly? Or would you try to step aside? And if you did, what might the gods do to you?"

Tanya's titles for younger children include three stories about Flotsam and Jetsam; the young novel *Waking Merlin* and its sequel *Merlin's Apprentice;* and *The World's Bellybutton* and its sequel *The Kraken Snores*. Since 1992 Tanya has been part of Storybox Theatre, working alongside her husband Rod Burnett. She lives with her family in Devon.

You can find out more about Tanya and her books by visiting her website at www.tanyalandman.com

Books by the same author

Apache

For younger readers

Flotsam and Jetsam

Flotsam and Jetsam and the Stormy Surprise

Flotsam and Jetsam and the Grooof

Waking Merlin

Merlin's Apprentice

The World's Bellybutton

The Kraken Snores

To Sally

The Goldsmith's Daughter

TANYA LANDMAN

Tanya Landman

**WALKER
BOOKS**

This is a work of fiction. Names, characters, places and
incidents are either the product of the author's imagination
or, if real, used fictitiously.

First published 2008 by Walker Books Ltd
87 Vauxhall Walk, London SE11 5HJ

2 4 6 8 10 9 7 5 3

Text © 2008 Tanya Landman
Cover photograph: Blend Images/Alamy

Extract p. 7 from *The Conquest of Mexico*
by Hugh Thomas, published by Hutchinson.
Reprinted by permission of The Random House Group Ltd.

The right of Tanya Landman to be identified as author of this work
has been asserted by her in accordance with the Copyright, Designs
and Patents Act 1988

This book has been typeset in Cochin and ATVisigoth

Printed in the UK by CPI Bookmarque, Croydon, CR0 4TD

British Library Cataloguing in Publication Data:
a catalogue record for this book
is available from the British Library

ISBN 978-1-4063-0707-8

www.walkerbooks.co.uk

To Averil, for wielding her red pen so tactfully,
and with such razor-sharp precision

We only came to sleep
We only came to dream;
It is not true, no it is not true
That we came to live on earth.

Excerpt from a traditional Aztec verse

*W*hen I slid into this world, my tiny body gliding wetly across the floor of my father's house like a fish plucked from the lake, I was pronounced dead. I lay curled, stiff and silent as the mother who had borne me. Wrapped in a torn cloak, I was set aside for burning.

But something nudged my infant self into taking a sharp, indrawn breath and emitting the piercing wail that brought my father running to my rescue. In taking my first breath, not only did I confound Pachtic the midwife, challenging her wisdom and earning her unrelenting resentment; with that one gasping cry I defied the gods.

In later years, when the horizons of my world had shrunk to the hearth and courtyard of my home, and my range of daily tasks had narrowed to endless cleaning and sweeping, and the pounding of maize and rolling of tortillas, I delighted in hearing the tale of my birth repeated. Over and over again our nurse, Mayatl, told it to me as she wove lengths of coloured cloth. I clutched the story to my chest, thrilling with delicious terror that I had once, albeit unknowingly, performed an act of such daring. For it seemed to me then, as one dull chore was succeeded by another of even greater tedium, that I would never have the chance to do anything so courageous again.

I was born in the market district of Tlaltelolco, in the northern part of the great city of Tenochtitlán, which lay at the heart of the vast Aztec empire. Here dwelt our mighty emperor, Montezuma, whose controlling hand reached every land and touched the very edges of the earth; in whose smallest fingertip was contained the power of life or death over each and every race of men.

Our city was a well-ordered one, but my father had both gone against its traditions and offended his own family when he married my mother. A goldsmith by trade, he should have chosen his bride from amongst the daughters of those who lived in the region of Azcapotzalco, where he himself had been born and had grown to manhood, and where gold was fashioned into fine ornaments, figurines and jewellery.

But one spring morning, as he went to buy jade and turquoise in the great market square of Tlaltelolco, his gaze fell upon my mother. She was trading maize and squashes grown by her father on the shallow, mud-filled chinampa fields that edged the city and provided the fresh vegetables which fed the population.

My mother, so my father sometimes said, had a smile that could outshine the sun. Laughing at a joke told by her sister, she failed to lower her eyes immediately, as she should have done, when my father looked at her. And in that one unguarded moment, the bonds of love tied my father's heart to hers. He would have no other wife. Staying by her side all that morning and for many mornings after, he followed her from the market one day and presented himself as her suitor to her astounded father. Though it was ancient custom for a father to choose his daughter's husband, my grandfather had not objected to the match. How could a peasant complain about his child winning the prize of a goldsmith?

Their ceremony followed some months later. The priests had examined the sacred calendar and set a day when the stars were best aligned to bring good fortune to the marriage. A healthy boy was predicted as the first fruit of their union.

My father's parents refused to come to the wedding, heartily disapproving of his choice of bride. Indeed, no other goldsmiths attended, for they would not mingle with peasant farmers. And yet the ceremony was a joyous occasion, full of laughter, my grandfather telling all who would listen how his clever daughter had traded sweet potatoes for a rich husband.

As my mother and father knelt on the matted floor, their cloaks were drawn together and the knot was tied that bound them as man and wife. And with that my mother's fate was sealed.

Ten months later – in the black of night while the sun battled against the dark spirits of the under-world – my mother fought her own desperate battle to bring me into the world. Pachtic the midwife chanted prayers to Tlazolteotl, the goddess of child-birth, and laid a warm stone on my mother's heaving belly to ease her pain. But nothing, neither prayers nor soothing herbs, could help her distress. When I finally came forth, sliding across the floor in a blue and bloodied mess, my mother slipped for a while into unconsciousness. She did not hear Pachtic's cry of disgust – first on seeing that I was a girl, and then on thinking that I was dead. It was not worth the trouble of reviving me: a girl was of no value. I was bundled away into a corner and Pachtic turned her attention back to my mother.

A swift examination showed that she carried more than one child. With a fervent prayer that this second baby would prove to be the promised boy, Pachtic began once more to aid my mother in her labour.

A short time later, drawing her knees to her chest in a last great spasm of pain, my mother fell again into unconsciousness. That last spasm ejected my brother from her dying body, but his large size tore her beyond recovering. He came feet first, as though prepared to stand and fight the instant he entered this world.

While Mayatl wiped my mother's brow and chafed her hands, frantically trying to hold her spirit in her body, Pachtic cut my brother's cord and safely stored it, for when he grew to adulthood he would have to carry it to a distant battlefield and bury it there. Pachtic bathed him with reverent prayers and ceremony in the cleansing waters that are the gift of Tlaloc, the rain god. Only after this ritual was my father allowed to have sight of his son.

But my father did not glance at the child who had seemingly killed his wife. Seeing his beloved's limp body he gave an anguished cry and, crouching low beside her, lifted her head to his breast and sobbed her name.

"Yecyotl!"

She heard him, for her eyes fluttered open, and her lovely smile greeted him fleetingly, before her soul at last departed.

Perhaps it was her spirit giving a soft, farewell caress that caused me then to wail.

"For I cried," I said, grinding my stone against maize.

"You cried." Mayatl spoke the words that had become chorus-like in the oft-repeating of them. "You were not to be disposed of so lightly. Small and weak though you were, you yelled, and a more indignant noise I have never heard!"

"And my father leapt up, and ran..."

"Your father ran, and cradled you in his arms, weeping."

"And he named me..."

"He named you for the thing you then were. Itacate, a little bundle of cloth – and his most precious possession."

In later years I realized that Mayatl had sweetened the tale for my hearing. My mother had passed from life to death as I had made the reverse journey. My father had clutched me, hoping, perhaps, that I carried a last word from her fleeing spirit. When he saw I was nothing more than a mortal baby – hungry, and demanding noisily to be fed – he handed me to Mayatl and looked at me no more.

The knowledge that my father had once held me was a bright jewel which I kept in my heart throughout my childhood years: a prize that was counterweight to the jealousy I sometimes had of my brother.

His bathing ceremony was held with great feasting and celebration four days after his birth. For he was born at the first dawn of Izcalli – the month of resurrection. At the precise moment that the sun broke free of the underworld and rose above the horizon, my brother entered this world. As the priests lifted their conch shells and gave the blast which called that morning into being, he took his first breath. The divine influences then were so propitious that the priests declared he was destined for deeds of glory. He would honour the gods and bring fame to his family.

The priests had studied the sacred calendar, and declared my brother's fate to be that of a mighty warrior: one who would shine above his fellow men and delight the gods with many captives. So when Pachtic laid the basin of water upon the reed mat, she placed beside it an amaranth-dough tortilla to

15

represent a shield, and set a small bow and arrow on top. He was named Mitotiqui, for the great uproar he would cause amongst our enemies when he faced them in battle.

Throughout the ritual of bathing and cleansing and prayers, I was tucked away in a dark corner. And when the feasting and music began, there I remained, attended only by Mayatl, never even glanced at by the guests who stood grouped at opposite ends of the house – goldsmiths and farmers keeping as far apart from each other as they could.

My own ceremony a few days later was a cursory affair, performed by Pachtic with perfunctory ritual. I was a girl, born under an ill-favoured sky. Though I had preceded my brother by just a few heartbeats, I had arrived before the dawn, in the dead days between years, when nothing good could be predicted.

The same priests who promised earthly distinction and eternal glory to my brother sucked their teeth and shook their heads over my small frame when called upon to determine my fate. One said I would not survive my infancy; another that my father's prayers would buy me a longer life, but it would be utterly unremarkable. The third – the most respected of the priesthood – was gloomier still. After long thought and much consumption of the sacred mushroom, he

16

made a terrible pronouncement. Not only would my life be worthless, but I would also bring ill fortune to all those closest to me. Any whose life brushed against mine was likely to be stained with it. And when I passed from this life to the next, I would not join my mother in the western paradise but would descend to the perpetual night of Mictlan with all those who lived dull, purposeless lives, and died fruitless, dishonourable deaths.

It was this prediction that everyone remembered. It was this that was whispered behind raised hands wherever I went. The gods had decided I could hope for nothing; I could expect nothing; I would do nothing. As a child, my fate weighed about my neck like a chain. But as I grew, so did a fierce determination that I would one day prove the priests and the gods wrong.

2

*W*ith the great difference in our fortunes it was small wonder that my love for Mitotiqui was tinged with bitterness. Perhaps it was more surprising that I loved him at all. But love him I did, with a sister's passionate devotion.

In our early years our father was so dazed, so deadened with sorrow at our mother's death, that we rarely approached him. He walked like a ghost through our lives: unseeing, unhearing, unfeeling. He ate; he slept; he worked. That was all. Each morning he went without a word to his workshop, and soon the smell of burning charcoal and melting gold would reach our nostrils. I longed to observe him at his craft – for even then I felt its lure – but never dared ask him. Our house was a silent one; and though we often heard music and cheerful conversation from the homes of our neighbours, our father avoided all contact with them.

We saw my mother's family rarely, for they were peasants; and besides, my grandfather's work was long and hard. He was as firmly fastened to his patch of soil as the willows that bordered his chinampa fields were rooted to the lake floor. Even had we wished to visit him, he would have had little time for us.

Mayatl was efficient. She fed us, bathed us, kept us clean and clothed. But she was our nurse, not our mother. Her duties ended with our bodily needs. Caresses were infrequent, and endearments – if they came – were awkward and uncomfortable.

And so Mitotiqui and I clung to one another, bestowing the affection that would have been our parents' due on each other. He was my companion, my playmate, one half of my soul. We learnt to stand by pushing ourselves up from the floor with hands on each other's shoulders. We took our first faltering steps with arms clasped tight about one another's necks. We learnt to run with fingers interlaced, so we might catch each other if we stumbled. We played in the sunlit courtyard of our home. If Mayatl tired of our noise and grew irritable, we would flee to the chinampa fields.

Here we learnt to swim, launching ourselves

across the clear water that divided the cultivated squares. Here, hidden amongst the verdant maize, I felt some relief from the heavy gaze of the gods, for they stared at me constantly: from the eyes of our household idols; from the painted statues carved at the foot of temples; from the murals that adorned the walls of the bathhouse. From every surface in the city they seemed to look with disdain upon this ill-omened child.

Amongst the lushly growing crops we would stare at the distant mountains that framed the lake. From beyond those hills came many merchants: traders of different races who displayed their wares in the marketplace where our parents had met.

"From there comes amber," Mitotiqui said, pointing east.

"And from there, gold," I suggested, pointing west.

"From there, jade and turquoise."

"Obsidian."

"Cotton."

"Salt."

"Slaves."

"Feathers."

As small children we often played this game, laughing, spinning, pointing, until we dizzied ourselves with it. Sometimes we fell to inventing all manner of strange, exotic goods and even stranger people who fashioned them.

"Two-headed men live in that direction. Their women lay eggs!"

"Eggs?"

"Yes, eggs! Huge orange ones that they bring to sell in the market. Crack them open and the yolks are deepest blue."

"Behind that hill live the tree dwellers. They sleep wrapped around branches like serpents, and swallow merchants whole who venture off the path."

"Beyond that valley live those who are half man, half bird. Their bellies are covered in feathers. They have beaks in place of noses and long tails on their behinds!"

As I became older, I yearned to see the lands that lay over the horizon. I longed to explore the empire to its very limits – to see the salted sea that circled the earth even as the lake circled our city. More, I wished to go beyond, to set forth in a canoe and peer over the edge where the waters met the sky and tumbled into the endless darkness of the underworld below.

But one day I realized that while my brother could, if he wished, see those unknown places and learn their secrets, I could not. I was a girl: the direction of my life would not be mine to choose. Thereafter the game lost its savour. We played it no more.

3

We were perhaps three years old when we first saw our warriors set forth for battle. It was an annual spectacle, but Mayatl had feared to attend when we were smaller lest we be lost in the crowd and crushed underfoot, for it was a ceremony of passionate grandeur which many thousands gathered to watch. My brother and I having grown sufficiently robust, she ventured to take us into the city's great temple precinct to witness the event.

It was the season of war. Each year, the same ritual was conducted, the same formal courtesies observed. Messengers were sent to the neighbouring land of Tlaxcala since this state alone refused to pay tribute to Montezuma, our emperor. They preferred instead this yearly battle, and Montezuma did not object, for our warriors brought many captives home for sacrifice. Full well I knew that the gods must have blood. It was knowledge that came with the first indrawn breath to one born in the Aztec empire. The reasons were many. To feed the sun and give it strength to do nightly battle in the underworld and rise once more. To make the rain fall; the seasons change; the maize grow. The earth gives of her own body to feed us; her own blood is the sweet water that we drink. It is fitting that her sacrifice be repaid. Blood alone delays the coming of the world's calamitous end, and in this season of battle it was the captured Tlaxcalans who would provide it.

Word had been given to their leaders. The ceremonial gifts and tokens had been sent. Accepted. The time was come.

My brother and I woke before sunrise, and lay waiting for the priests to call forth the dawn upon their conch shells. When the first blast came from the city's principal temple it sounded faint, but spreading outwards from temple to temple it became louder until it reached the one in our own district of Tlaltelolco some small distance away. It was soon followed by the tread of bare feet on stone as slaves went into the streets: some to sweep, some to carry food and hot charcoal braziers to the temple priests who would be letting their own blood in reverent ritual to feed the rising sun.

At once Mitotiqui and I leapt from our reed mats and began to dress, falling over ourselves and each other in our haste.

Our house was neither so grand as those of other goldsmiths, nor so plain as the mud-brick peasants' huts that stood facing us across the canal. There were four rooms, stone built, opening onto a large courtyard. My father's chamber gave access to a second, smaller square, at the rear of which stood his workshop.

My brother and I slept in the smallest chamber at that time, as did Mayatl, a reed screen giving her a little privacy. At the sound of our chatter she began to stir, grumbling at our eagerness.

Mayatl took longer to ready herself than we did, for while our childish locks hung loose about our shoulders, she had to braid her tresses in the elaborate manner of older women. Impatiently we waited, hopping restlessly from foot to foot, though we attempted to hold our tongues, for we did not wish to disturb our father. When she was done, we crossed the courtyard together to the kitchen.

Before cooking, before eating, before doing anything, Mayatl knelt low, touching her forehead to the floor in front of the recessed shrine that held our idols. From the sixty deities honoured by our priests in the rites and rituals of the sacred year, the head of each household must choose which he will single out for personal devotion. My father revered Quetzalcoatl, maker of mankind and patron of artists and goldsmiths; Tlaltecuhtli, earth goddess and protector of hearth and home; and Tezcatlipoca, who grants fortune to those he favours, ill luck to those he does not. My father's prayers to Tezcatlipoca were heartfelt pleas to lessen or delay the disaster that the predictions warned I would bring.

Our idols were not moulded from clay or carved from wood but cast in gold by the hand of my father. Their jewelled eyes stared, pressing me to the floor in humble veneration.

When our prayers were over, Mayatl blew on the embers that glowed in the brazier and roused them back to life. In their heat she set a vessel of broth she had prepared the previous day, and handed us each a small piece of tortilla. We could eat but little as our bellies were so full of excitement. When we had finished, Mayatl led us out into the city.

The sun had not yet climbed above the mountains, and though the eastern sky glowed faint pink, the streets were drab in the grey light. The cool air was still heavy with night perfumes that would fade in the growing heat of day. While we passed between houses, the sweet scent of tobacco flowers and lime filled our nostrils. As we neared a temple, the aroma of blossom was lost in the rich tang of slaves' burning hearts that smouldered in sacrifice on the altar.

We were not alone. Despite the earliness of the hour, many people were hastening to the centre of the city where the warriors would soon be gathered. Mayatl took one of our hands in each of hers and dragged Mitotiqui and me behind her. Eager though we were, we struggled to keep pace and were quite breathless when at last we reached the principal temple.

It was the first time I had seen it this close. It was higher than any other pyramid in Tenochtitlán and could be seen from every district, including my own, so I was familiar with its outline. But I had not realized until we entered the square how tall it was. It punctured the sky! The sun itself could pause and rest on its peak!

I stood, staring in delighted wonder, moving only when Mayatl's tug pulled me into the crowd that milled in the precinct and jerked us towards the temple itself. So overwhelmed was I that I would not set foot upon the holy steps until Mayatl lifted me, hoisting me aloft and setting me on a stone plinth so that I could see above the heads and watch all that happened. Mitotiqui was beside me. I saw my own astonishment reflected in his face. For once, we were quiet. Awe burned all words from our minds.

And then came the warriors.

Six abreast, they marched in three columns, the people dividing to let them through. They halted in front of the palace, which faced the temple from across the square, and there awaited the coming of the emperor.

At the rear stood the ordinary soldiers, dressed in quilted cotton armour. Stiffly proud yet awkward, their bearing spoke more of fear than of courage. In the season of peace a man cannot change his allotted place, but by proving excellence in battle he may rise from the peasantry to the elite. Those whose hair hung loose were the untried sons of farmers hoping for such elevation. In front of them were grouped those who had fought in previous wars and were permitted to tie their hair in the esteemed warriors' topknot.

Before this group stood the jaguar knights, clad in yellow, blackly spotted skins, their own heads covered by the skulls of the beasts, their faces peering out from between bared teeth. Painted shields trimmed with iridescent feathers were fixed on their left arms. Obsidian-bladed cudgels dangled idle in their right hands.

Heading the force were the eagle knights, decked in savagely beaked costumes. Designed to terrify an enemy, their fearsome aspect was enough to fill my head with nightmares for many weeks to come.

On seeing the warriors, Mitotiqui shouted in excitement, "I shall be dressed like them! Soon! Soon! And then you will shake before me, sister!"

Furious, I struck him, earning a sharp reprimand from Mayatl. Before I could protest, a sudden hush gripped the crowd. There was a stirring from the palace. Many slaves hastened onto the flat roof, walking backwards, bent low until they reached the far side. There was a breathless silence. And then our emperor came forth.

At that moment, the sun crested the distant hills, and instantly the square was flooded with light. It illuminated the palace, making the whitewashed walls dazzle as though gilded with silver. It touched the brilliant blue flowers of morning glory that spilt from the roof, caressing them with warmth until they sprang open as if in response to the emperor's presence. The orange blooms of climbers that twined upwards from the ground raised their heads to bask in his splendour.

Montezuma wore a magnificent headdress, the emerald-green tail feathers of the sacred quetzal fanning out in a wide circle. His cloak was of gleaming white, and his body seemed more clad in gold than cloth, so many were the jewels that bedecked his person.

As one, the crowd had lowered their heads and knelt, for it is forbidden to look upon the lord of the world and to do so meant death. I was slow to respond. Before my head was forced down by a furious Mayatl, I glimpsed the glory of Montezuma. I beheld his power, and my child's heart swelled with pride that I should dwell in the same city as he who ruled the world.

His words when they came carried to the ears of all those gathered in the square below him.

"The seasons have turned, the sacred calendar has moved, and once more it is the time for war. Go forth to our enemy. Face the battle to come with courage. If the gods see fit that you are taken captive, then die with joy in your heart. You shall walk for ever in paradise. Do not step back from the fight. Never retreat. Death. Glory. These two alone are your choices. You are men of Tenochtitlán! You are favoured by the gods! Do them honour and they shall bring you fame. Bring many home for sacrifice!"

A screaming shout from the priests' throats answered him. Many drums began to beat, and the crowd chanted, thousands lifting their voices in veneration of the warriors. The priests moved amongst the columns of men, sprinkling their chests with blood to buy the favour of Huitzilopochtli, god of war, the deity most revered by our emperor.

With great ceremony the warriors turned away from the palace and began to march towards the wide causeway that joined our city to the distant shore. A cry of exultation erupted from the onlookers. Mothers clasped daughters to their breasts, their ardent prayers begging the gods to send an honourable destiny for their sons and brothers. Fathers watched, chins held high.

Tears coursed down Mayatl's face as she caught the crowd's stirring emotion. Seeing her expression, I looked sideways at my brother. But though Mitotiqui was turned towards me, his eyes did not meet mine. They followed the eagle knights. As his lips curled into a smile, I felt a stab of jealous pain. My brother was viewing his own glorious future.

4

When Mitotiqui and I were nine years old, a strange sight appeared in the night sky that sent tremors of apprehension quivering throughout Tenochtitlán.

The festival of Miquiztli, held in honour of our dead ancestors, was upon us. In previous years Mayatl had acquired the flowers we needed from the market, judging us too small and too foolish to gather our own. But Mitotiqui had grown so much during the preceding winter that his head was now touching her shoulder. At my urging, he asked that we be allowed to leave the city. Pursing her lips, with many stern warnings that we were to behave respectfully, she at last fastened a bundle of provisions on my brother's back. With an empty basket balanced upon her head, Mayatl led us from our home towards the distant hills.

In ancient times the gods had guided our ancestors through the wilderness to the great lake valley in which we lived. Our forefathers had diverted streams and drained marshes, building temples and palaces on the islands they reclaimed from the water god and linking them with ornate bridges and level causeways. From nothing, they had made Tenochtitlán, and from Tenochtitlán they had set forth to conquer, creating the Aztec empire that now covered the entire world.

There were three causeways across the lake that joined our city to the shore beyond. To reach the nearest to our home, we had first to pass through the great market square of Tlaltelolco.

It was impossible for Mitotiqui and me to enter the market without looking hopefully towards the slave traders. It was the custom that if a slave escaped, he could be pursued only by his seller. If he could flee as far as the palace and touch its walls, he would gain his freedom.

On this day, no such excitement gave us diversion. There were no slaves grouped miserably in the corner. Instead, the whole square was brimful of bright blooms. Deep reds, fiery oranges, rich purples. Flowers of every shape and hue were piled high on reed mats, and their sellers called loudly to attract buyers. The air was heady with scents that thrilled the senses. Clutching us tightly, Mayatl dragged us through the throng.

It was scarcely less crowded on the causeway, which streamed with people heading in both directions. A sharp shout of greeting and there before us was Pachtic the midwife. She at once embraced Mitotiqui, squeezing his plump cheek as though he were a sun-ripe fruit. I smiled at her but received no such token of affection. Instead she brushed past me, drawing aside her cloak as if to prevent its being soiled with ill fortune.

We wove our way along the causeway, bare feet treading carefully on the timber that bridged each section of stone. After a mile or so we reached the land, and I looked about me with interest. As Tenochtitlán had grown, its population had spilt beyond the city to the lake shore. A small town had sprung up here at the causeway's end. I had often seen the outlines of these buildings – on a clear day the distant temple pyramid and dwellings were a familiar sight. But to now be amongst them, to cross the paved square and follow the wide streets to the hills, was an odd sensation, akin to walking into a painting daubed upon a wall. Strangest of all was to feel so much grass beneath my feet. I, who had only ever walked on sun-warmed stone and terracotta tiles, or in the soft dampness of the chinampa fields, found the dry, scratchy unevenness at once peculiarly uncomfortable and wildly exhilarating.

When we reached the open hillside, Mitotiqui, basking in the sunshine like a well-fed dog, was content to remain at Mayatl's side and lazily pluck an occasional bloom from the grass. I was not. Fearing what lay beyond but unable to resist its pull, I edged slowly towards the crest of the hill, taking my basket with me in pretence of searching for bigger and brighter petals. But I had not climbed to the peak – I was not even close to it – when Mayatl's harsh tones called me back. Admonishing me, she sent me down the slope of the hill below her. I was hemmed in: the town to one side, Mayatl to the other, where she could see easily if I attempted to stray.

After a morning's picking we ate the tortillas and tomatoes that Mayatl had packed as a noonday meal. Sitting in the prickly grass, pestered by biting insects, we looked down at our city. Ringed with mountains on all sides, it seemed to be suspended in the centre of the lake, its buildings silvered by the bright sun. When we walked its streets it felt vast – an endless maze of dwellings and temples. But now, for the first time, I could see it in its entirety. And for the first time, I could measure its limits.

✤   ✤   ✤

34

With baskets brimming, and arms full of flowers that were already wilting in the heat, we returned across the causeway.

Each district of Tenochtitlán has its own temples for daily worship. But for the important festivals that mark each year's cycle, all flock to the principal temple in the central square. Once through the narrow streets of Tlaltelolco, we joined the throng passing along a broad avenue towards the heart of the city.

Throughout the year, the steps of the temple ran red with the blood of sacrifice. But for the festival of Miquiztli, they were coloured scarlet with flowers. The pyramid was festooned with fragrant blooms, petals rippling in the spring breeze, each one representing one of the departed dead. The priests say that on this earth we are all flowers who wither and die within a few, fleeting moments.

On reaching the base of the temple, we began to climb carefully amongst the blooms, ascending steadily until we saw the whole network of canals and streets spread out below us. There we placed our flowers reverently on the steps.

The throbbing beat of drums and pipes sounded beneath us in the square; and as we watched, the crowd cleared, standing back from the space in which the men would dance.

When at last we joined the onlookers, I searched for my father amongst the whirling figures, and saw that as he danced his brow was knitted with pain. He had not ceased regretting that my mother had stayed with him for so short a time, and this, the festival of the dead, was an annual reminder of his loss. Even at nine years old, I watched him with fear in my heart, mutely pleading for him to mask his expression, for it was unwise to offend the priests. They moved through the crowd, their hair matted, their faces stained black, their ears lacerated by each morning's offering of their own blood. I knew well that if any of them noticed the terrible heartache shown so clearly on my father's face, they would look upon him with displeasure. For we are taught that the life we have on earth is nothing but a passing dream, soon over. Death opens the door to reality and we must all meet it without fear or sadness.

In the press of the great crowd that had gathered, I felt Mitotiqui's hand squeeze my own. I did not need to meet his eyes to know what he suggested. As one we turned, weaving between those who penned us in, and ran for the fields. We knew chastisement from Mayatl would come later for our unruly flight, but the draw of sunshine and freedom was irresistible.

We raced through the broad streets and narrow

alleys, past the steam baths where men and women went to chatter and gossip, meeting no one but slaves sweeping the streets, for all were gathered in the square to witness the ritual dance. At last, breathless and giggling, we sat on a narrow footbridge that joined the fields, our dangling toes attracting the attention of several large fish that circled below.

Perhaps recollection of our mother made him thoughtful, for suddenly Mitotiqui heaved a sigh and looked back at the shimmering city. Dropping a flower into the water, he said softly, "They say this life isn't real."

"I know what they say," I replied, dipping my toe in the water and watching a fish give it an inquisitive bite. I had heard the priests' words often enough. And yet my child's mind had difficulty in grasping their meaning. The world felt solid to me; I could imagine no other reality. I scooped a handful of water and threw it at Mitotiqui, but his sudden seriousness was not to be so easily shaken.

"I wonder what paradise is like?" he mused.

My brother lifted his chin to the heavens and smiled. I could see his mind exploring the happy prospect of eternal bliss, and I was filled with such resentment that I had to grit my teeth to stop spiteful words from tumbling out. I lowered my eyes and stared angrily into the lake, shivering, although the day had not yet grown cold. It seemed Mitotiqui had forgotten that in death we would be divided. He would walk on clouds in the vaulted sky above, while I would spend eternity beneath the earth in the black gloom of Mictlan.

My brother was dazzling, as light and as radiant as the sun. But sometimes, when he smiled as he did then, his very brightness seemed to throw me into shadow. At those times I felt as though I were indeed a dark-hearted, ill-favoured creature, cursed by the gods.

We returned home late, disgruntled and irritated with one another as children sometimes are. Mayatl's words of reprimand further inflamed me, and I settled to sleep too heated with anger to take any proper rest.

So I was awake, gazing through the open doorway at the stars, when the sky suddenly became light. It was not the beginning of a new day; I knew well that the sun had barely begun its battle with the night and that the dawn – if it came – was still many hours away. And yet the central courtyard of our house was filled with a strange amber glow. I rose, and went into the street.

I was not alarmed. For those first moments, when I stood alone beneath the sky, I was enraptured by the beauty of the sight that greeted me. A plume of fire as tall as the principal temple burned in the very heart of the heavens. Shaped like a grain of corn, from it many small flames fell earthwards like tears – or drops of blood.

I watched in wonder, until the scream of a woman rang from a nearby house, and my father was roused from his slumber. A commotion followed as one by one all the residents of the district woke to this strange vision and spilt, befuddled and dishevelled, from their houses into the street. Mayatl sent me back inside, telling me to remain safely with my brother, but we could no more stay within than we could fly. When her back was turned, we slipped out and joined the throng of people who stared skywards.

Whispers spread and fear grew like a wind-whipped wave upon the lake, starting with a little ripple but rising higher and higher until at last there was an outcry of terrified confusion. None could agree the precise meaning of the sight but all seemed certain of one thing.

The flame was a warning of some terrible disaster to come.

I did not sleep that night. At my father's command my brother and I returned to our chamber and lay still. But when Mayatl's breathing slowed and we knew she slept, we whispered to each other of what we had seen.

We lived in the age of the fifth sun.

When the fourth sun had perished in a great flood, the gods Tezcatlipoca and Quetzalcoatl had fashioned new land and sky from the body of the earth goddess. But the deities stood in darkness until the resplendent Tecuciztécatl offered himself to be a new sun. Nanahuatzin, a smaller god whose disfigured face was studded with pimples and open sores, also volunteered for the honour of lighting the new-made earth.

Both prepared themselves with rites of penitence, just as a new emperor does when he comes to the throne. Then the other gods prepared a vast, flaming pyre and the splendid Tecuciztécatl made lavish offerings of sweet-smelling incense and the brightly coloured feathers of the sacred quetzal before it. But Nanahuatzin laid out something more simple: blood-covered thorns with which he had pierced his own body.

Both gods approached the fire. Tecuciztécatl was driven back by the dreadful heat. Four times he tried, but he had neither the courage nor the will to enter the flames. Without fear the scarred, imperfect Nanahuatzin stepped into the pyre; and, as his earthly body burned to ashes, the fifth sun was born. Shamed by his own cowardice, Tecuciztécatl also threw himself on the flames. He became the pale moon.

The earth was lit, but the fifth sun hung exhausted and motionless in the heavens. Only when the gods cut their bodies, feeding him with their own hearts' blood, did he have the strength to move across the sky.

Thus the age of the fifth sun dawned. With blood. With sacrifice.

With death.

And – so the priests foretold – it would draw to a close with earthquakes and destruction.

By that strange light Mitotiqui and I clasped each other for comfort, trembling in fear of what was to come.

Full well we knew that the age into which we had been born would end in fire.

The flame blazed in the sky all that night, and the many nights that followed. For almost a year the spectacular omen hung above us. To begin with, fear held the city in its icy fingers, but when month followed month and no disaster came, it waned. Though it did not entirely vanish, it was put away in a dark corner, where it could be overlooked and ignored.

I grew accustomed to the warm glow that filled our courtyard, and it gave me comfort. The night was a time of terror when the sun battled for its very life, and all feared lest it failed in its struggle and rose no more. So when at last the strange sky fire faded and ceased I missed it sorely, for the night seemed darker and blacker than it had ever been. Whether it was truly so, or whether my troubled heart and bitter thoughts coloured my perception, it was impossible to tell. For when the omen vanished, Mayatl decided it was time I learnt to weave.

I was then ten years old, and had been aiding her in the household tasks since I was four – a little later than most girls, who assisted their mothers almost as soon as they could walk. As a small child, my weak stature had bought me a time of freedom. But when I survived my early childhood, and racing against my brother had made me grow strong, I became condemned to a life of domesticity.

It had started with sweeping and scrubbing, tasks I did not greatly object to, for they gave me access to my father's workshop. When he was absent I was sent there by Mayatl to dust and sweep, but I spent more time examining his designs and handling polished gems than I ever did in cleaning. Secretly, alone, I learnt the weight of fine stones and observed the flaws that marred those of lesser value. I studied the settings he worked, seeing how they displayed the gems to their best advantage.

But the goldsmith's art was not for me. Girls could not be craftsmen. At seven, I had to learn the art of cooking tortillas.

My first attempt had been a disaster. I had rushed the grinding of the maize, being too hasty with the heavy stone to produce a smooth flour. Likewise,

I had hurried the shaping and rolling of the dough, so desperate had I been to finish the chore and get back to Mitotiqui. I recall my father chewing bravely on the hard, lumpen tortilla, saying nothing but smiling vaguely with encouragement until he gave a sudden cry and clutched his jaw.

It seemed I had done my task so poorly that a piece of grit had become mingled with the grain and chipped his tooth. My heart had beaten fast with shame for many days as his mouth swelled in wordless accusation. He had finally had his tooth pulled, and, although he never once reproached me, I made a solemn vow then to cause him no further injury. I would be careful. But the dreariness of grinding corn was an endless source of irritation to me. And I burned with jealousy that while I knelt rolling the stone back and forth, Mitotiqui was allowed to follow my father and assist him when he worked gold into fine ornaments.

Mitotiqui was destined for glory on the field of battle, but a warrior is not always at war. Only in the appropriate season did our army set forth to fight the ancient enemy, Tlaxcala. Therefore my father reasoned that Mitotiqui also needed to learn the goldsmith's art.

Envy of my brother soured my temper. I had not forgotten my stolen glimpse of the emperor's adornments. Indeed, each time I set foot in the city streets I could not help but glance at nobles to assess the craftsmanship of the jewels they wore. Tortilla-making seemed such dull, repetitious labour in comparison. To relieve the tedium I often moulded shapes in the dough – the gods, the tiny hairless dogs that were the pets of noblemen, the flowers that tumbled from the roof of every house – before I had to squash them and roll the dough flat. Such usage did not improve the flavour of my tortillas, nor soften their texture. I was a pitifully poor cook, for I saw no reward in the task. Hour after hour I pummelled and flattened and baked, only to see my work disappear in the course of a single meal!

I complained of it crossly to Mitotiqui. "What our father crafts – what you craft – will last for ever. Anything I make vanishes down your throat in the blink of an eye!"

"You think so?" Mitotiqui's voice was deadly serious, but his eyes gleamed teasingly. "I assure you, Itacate, you are mistaken."

"How?"

"Your tortillas are so heavy that they take months to pass through my insides." He rubbed his stomach. "In fact, I think there is one lodged just here that you baked last year."

I cried with indignation, and cuffed Mitotiqui as

he mimed chewing, and gave a perfect imitation of my father smashing his tooth.

"Your tortillas are good, solid creations. They are immortal, Itacate, like the gods." He nudged me. "Perhaps our emperor should use them to pave his palace. They would last longer than terracotta."

I fell upon him in play, beating him around the head with the palm of my hand. And so, with laughter, my brother lightened the weight of my domestic burden. But even he could not ease my horror of weaving, for by then he was attending school.

I was ten. In five or six years my father would approach Nemaneoanoliztli, the matchmaker, and she would begin the search to find me a suitable husband. It went unsaid, but I knew well that a good match was unlikely to be made: the predictions at my birth made certain of that. Nevertheless, Mayatl was determined that I should learn all the womanly skills that would be expected of a wife.

My life acquired a deadly, dull discipline. Mornings were taken up with grinding maize and cooking, sweeping and cleaning. The rest of the daylight hours were spent spinning and weaving. We had a constant need of cloth not only for clothing, but also for bartering at market. Well-woven fabric could be exchanged for meat and vegetables.

When Mayatl first fitted me to the loom, I felt

as though a huge chain were being fastened about my waist, pinning me to the hearth. The strap was passed behind my back and tied to the first bar of wood. Mayatl then tied the second – the loom bar – to a post in the courtyard. Here I was to kneel, using my weight to straighten the warp threads that ran between the two bars. Inside that contraption I felt as helpless and trapped as a trussed chicken.

Mayatl then showed me how to pass the weft thread over and under the strands of warp, using a heddle stick and shed rod to lift the alternating strands. With a steadily sinking heart, I began. I knelt until my neck ached, my fingers were raw, my knees had lost all feeling, and the sun had sunk into the darkness of Mictlan. Back and forth I passed the heddle, over and under, thread by tiny, narrow, hair-thin thread.

At the end of that first day, in the still darkness while the rest of the city slept, I wept. I felt I could work all year and still see only a fingernail's length of fabric! And if I wanted to follow the design that was Mayatl's instruction, I did not know how I would endure it. It was so complex, and yet so repetitive! I could not even talk, or listen to Mayatl's tales, for the concentration I needed was so great. Not even the story of my birth could relieve the tedium of the task.

As day succeeded day, month followed month and the years moved on, I became more skilled, but I grew to loathe the cloths I created. They were so flat. So dull. So unvarying. I dreaded the moment after the noonday meal when we had finished eating, and I could avoid my loom no longer. Each piece I wove seemed to drain me of energy, of spirit, of life. I dreamt of fabric, the patterns dancing before my eyes even when the lids were shut.

To evade this domestic oppression I began more and more to retreat to a place deep inside my head. Into my cloths I threaded stories of escape. The heddle stick became myself – weaving between the reeds at the edge of the lake, between boulders as I climbed the hills, between stout trunks of trees in distant jungles. When I beat the weft threads into position, I journeyed further away. By the time each piece was finished, in my mind I had arrived amongst a strange new tribe of men, and I was weaving freely amongst them in a great, triumphant dance.

While I stayed, bound with tight cords of resentment to my loom, my brother was schooled. He went not to the telpochcalli, where the son of a goldsmith might be expected to attend, but to the calmecac along with the city's nobility, for his propitious birth had marked him for great deeds. Here he excelled both in learning and in popularity, as the gods had blessed Mitotiqui with a spirit that charmed everyone he met.

Each day I eagerly awaited his return; I found our home empty and lifeless without him and our daily separation miserably hard to endure. I had always thought us to be two halves of one whole, and in his absence I felt myself to be a shrivelled, withered thing. When he came back, he would sit with me awhile, telling me of what he had learnt. His world had expanded as mine shrank, and I devoured his knowledge with the same fervour as he devoured his food.

One afternoon he returned home wielding a cudgel, a fearsome, flat-sided weapon with many sharp obsidian blades set into the edges. In high spirits he demonstrated to me the elaborate steps of the ritual dance that preceded any battle.

"And then I must approach my enemy thus," he declared, grimacing menacingly.

I laughed at his expression, as he intended I should.

"Can you not just beat your opponent over the head?" I asked. "Would it not be a swifter way to dispatch him?"

Mitotiqui sighed dramatically. "The object is not

to kill, Itacate, as well you know. I must take live captives for sacrifice." He swung his cudgel again.

"You are likely to remove their legs if you do it like that," I replied. "Then how will they climb the temple steps?"

"Wait and see, Itacate. The blood I take shall make the sun rise. I am an important man. Do not forget it."

He spoke in jest, but his remark grated, setting my teeth on edge.

As children we had always talked as equals. Fool that I was, I had expected it to remain so. We had always delighted in flights of fancy, each of us striving to top the other with the wildness of our imaginings. But now our conversation was lopsided. Daily my brother came back with tales of new triumphs and nuggets of knowledge that gleamed like gold. And what could I tell Mitotiqui in return?

He would say, "Today we studied the movement of the stars and assessed the sacred calendar. And then we practised the skills of oratory, debating whether the gods are separate deities, or aspects of one vast whole as the poet Nezahualcoyotl thought."

Was I to reply, "Today *I* studied the movement of the grinding stone and assessed the inordinate amount of time it takes to turn maize into flour. Then

I knelt for hours within my loom and debated with myself whether I should use the red or the black thread, and if anyone in the entire world would care a grain of salt either way"?

Mitotiqui perfected imitations of his fellow students and the many priests who taught him. He copied their speech and their way of walking with deadly accuracy. And how was I to entertain him in return? By mimicking the ant who carried a fragment of corn across the courtyard while I spun thread? By impersonating the spider who repaired its web above me with greater skill than I could ever master? For I neither met nor talked with anyone else!

I could say nothing. So while Mitotiqui became more eloquent, more glorious, more shining, as he grew to manhood, I became his opposite: tight-lipped, dark, dull. If we were parts of one whole, we were no longer twin halves. He was the corn's kernel, growing and ripening to perfect fruition; I was the husk – empty, dried out, discarded and useless. Thus it went on. Until the day I crossed him, and tainted his golden glow.

We were by that time fifteen years old. My brother had continued to assist our father in his workshop, and one evening he brought a necklet into the house to show me. It was Mitotiqui's own work – he had made it unaided – and he was proud of his craftsmanship.

I did not mean to be cruel, but as I examined it I realized his work was ill done: he had marred the beauty of the stones in setting them, rather than enhancing them.

I was out of sorts, or I would have chosen my words more carefully. I did not bother with soothing tact, but merely said, "It is badly made," and handed his work back to him.

Mitotiqui's brow furrowed, but only for a moment. He had become accustomed to my curtness and was not troubled. Besides, he had an open heart and a generous nature; if my criticism was just, he would accept it.

"You think so?" he asked. "How should it be done?"

I took the necklet once more and examined the stones. He had matched them with little thought to hue and shape, and I told him so. Several small flawed turquoises were embedded around a perfect jade of infinitely superior quality. The turquoises clashed with the jade, somehow draining it of colour. And as for the setting he had worked around them...

"Look at the jade," I said. "Feel its weight; see its shape. It should be framed by the gold, not weighed down by it. You have made it look as though … as though…" I struggled to find an apt description, but Mitotiqui supplied one for me.

"As though a bird's dropping has landed on it!"

I smiled at him, laughing. But then our father's voice slid like a knife between us.

"Quite so."

These words alarmed us as neither Mitotiqui nor I had heard his approach. We sprang apart guiltily, although why we did so was a puzzle, for we had done nothing wrong.

Our father studied our faces closely in the fading light. We had become so used to his indifference that such intensity was a frightening thing. Furtively I glanced at Mitotiqui, but his expression mirrored my own; neither of us knew what to say.

My father broke our silence. Crossing the room and taking my arm, he led me into the courtyard. Pointing at the ground he said, "There! Show me what you would have done with the jade."

It was a test, a challenge: one I did not wish to fail. My heart pounded. I did not know what my father meant by it, but I felt the moment was heavy with significance. I would not be hurried. I held the necklet in my hand and considered the jade. It was a perfect circle of smooth, even colour. How best to enhance its beauty? It should stand alone, of that

I was certain, not compete against other beads. Not a necklet, then… Perhaps a figurine?

While the sun's last rays streaked the sky blood red, I found a sharp stone and scratched the image of Tezcatlipoca, the god who brings fortune, on the terracotta tiles, the jade the mirror in which the god sees the future. It was hastily done, but not poorly. The shape I had drawn was elegant and apt.

My father expelled a long breath. Slowly he nodded his approval.

"You have the eye of a goldsmith!" he exclaimed, and his tone was one of wonder. He whispered, almost to himself, "My own seem to have been tight shut these many years." Then, grasping my chin in his hand, he softly spoke my name. "Itacate." A smile lifted the corners of his mouth as he looked at me, seemingly for the first time. "Child, you have the face of your mother!"

His voice was so unexpectedly tender that my vision was briefly blurred with tears. Wiping them away, I glanced at my brother to see his reaction to this strange scene.

Mitotiqui stood framed in the doorway, lit red by the dying light. He was struggling to compose his features, but I could read the emotion upon them. He – the glorious child whom the gods favoured – had never had cause to feel envy before, not of me, not of anyone. But now it burst into his heart with all the heated energy and raw strength of a new-made sun.

Brilliant. Fierce. Searing.

He turned away, for he did not know how to control his anguish. My own heart contracted and I felt then that I was cursed. It seemed bitter indeed that at the very moment my father had looked at me and seen something more than an ill-favoured daughter, my brother's face had become stained by the dark cloud of jealousy.

*I*t had taken my father fifteen years to recall that he had a daughter. It did not take him so long to make use of me.

The next market day, instead of going to the square with Mayatl as usual, I accompanied my father there, walking three steps behind him, head bowed, the very picture of a dutiful daughter. And this time I did not stop amongst the fresh fruit and vegetables. Instead I followed where he led, winding through stalls piled high with turkeys, deer, rabbits, fish. The smell of dead flesh jostled with the scents of heady oils and perfumes. My father led me past the sellers of pots and jars and bowls, and the vendors of fine cloaks and sandals. We did not pause to admire the bright displays of precious feathers laid out by Mayan traders, nor the skins of jaguar and panther spread on the ground by those of the Otomi tribe. My father walked, his eyes fixed on the far corner.

I knew where he led. As children, Mitotiqui and I had often evaded Mayatl's clutches and lost ourselves in this vast, crowded throng. Like moths to the moon we would always be drawn to the place where my father now took me. A canal ran along one side of the square. Heavily laden canoes banged against the stone quay, and each other, threatening to unbalance and capsize. At the furthest end merchants from the very edges of the world traded precious stones, silver and gold. Children are invisible to some adults' eyes, and we had spent many hours staring and giggling at the strange foreigners with their unfamiliar dialects and exotic dress.

Thinking about my brother now brought a stab of sorrow to my chest. Mitotiqui fought and struggled against his jealousy, but my father – all unknowing – poured salt in his wound with every word he spoke. At our evening meals, he had taken to bringing in pieces he had worked on during the day to show me how they had been made, and to ask my opinion of them. He did not ask for Mitotiqui's. Thrilled and flattered though I was to have our father's favour suddenly, I felt the pain it gave my brother. And so in the space of a few days our meals had become strained, uncomfortable affairs. I had never imagined that Mitotiqui's time in our father's workshop might have been as torturous to him as the loom was to me; he had never spoken of it. But then neither had I told him how much I hated my weaving. We were twins; we had shared the same womb. And yet now, how little we seemed to know of each other!

It was something of a relief to be in the marketplace with my father alone. Mitotiqui was in the calmecac that day. For now at least I did not have to juggle the bad feelings of one against the good opinion of the other.

As we approached the traders, they began to call out to my father.

"Oquitchli! See here! I have fine black obsidian – very rare."

"I have pearls from the distant shores – only the highest quality for you, Oquitchli."

"Oquitchli! I have an amber here that you would trade your mother for!"

My father gave a rueful laugh. We both knew he had not exchanged a word with his mother since his choice of bride had so offended her. "By all the gods, I believe I would trade her for a grain of salt!" he muttered to me. But he extended his hand for the amber and began to examine it.

It was a fine stone, and as my father turned it over my palms tingled with excitement. A piece of great splendour could be worked around such a jewel!

My father seemed pleased and began to talk over the price with Popotl the trader, first giving the stone to me. Popotl raised his eyebrows in surprise, but said nothing.

I weighed the gem, still warm from my father's touch, in my hand. It was beautiful, as large as a chicken's egg and suffused with a rich, honeyed glow. And yet a prickle stirred the hairs on my neck. Something was amiss. I held it to the light, examining it minutely. It seemed perfect, and yet some instinct told me to continue. I twisted it slowly in the sunlight, and – yes, I was right! A tiny fissure ran through the stone. If it was worked, the gem would crack in two.

My father was about to complete the transaction. I hesitated, not knowing how to speak in front of the trader, for I – a girl – should hold my tongue in the presence of men. I laid my hand upon my father's arm and gave a slight pull. He turned, frowning.

"Is something the matter, Itacate?" he said coldly.

"There is a flaw," I answered quietly.

"Show me."

My father studied the gem, holding it to the light as I had done, and then handed it back to the trader, saying, "Sadly, Popotl, your stone is blemished."

I kept my eyes lowered while Popotl examined his amber. After a long pause he spoke. "You are right, Oquitchli. I had not seen it. My most sincere apologies. I did not intend to sell you inferior goods." He bowed respectfully to my father, his glance flicking nervously towards the raised platform where the council was gathered. These men had the duty of overseeing the market, ensuring that all was sold in the correct place and at the correct price. Penalties for those caught cheating were high: a dishonest merchant would be shamed, perhaps even stoned, if his crime was great.

My father chose to believe Popotl's mistake was genuine. "No matter," he said. "What else can you show me?"

More stones were produced, and these my father also gave to me for my inspection. At last we purchased what he needed: nothing so spectacular as the amber, but all gems of fine quality.

We made our way through the crowds without speaking. Along the canal, over the bridge that spanned it. As we journeyed homewards, my father stopped walking and turned to face me.

"I did not see the fault in the amber," he said thoughtfully. "Indeed, I did not even know you were right until Popotl confirmed it."

I said nothing, but was astonished at my father's sudden trust in me. I also wondered with some alarm what would have happened if Popotl had not admitted the flaw.

"It seems your eyes see more than mine these days, Itacate. I think I must make use of them for grading the stones I work with. I would like your help for a short time in the mornings. Will you mind being taken from the kitchen?"

It was but a small lessening of my domestic burden, yet much discipline, much self-control, it took to prevent myself crying out with joy. I kept my eyes lowered until I could compose my features into a suitable expression.

"No, Father," I said humbly. "I shall be happy to aid you however you wish."

He nodded, content, and walked onwards. Again I followed, but now my blood thrilled. Sad though I was that my father's sight had dimmed with age, I felt like a slave who had touched the palace walls and gained freedom. To be invited into my father's workshop – to have my assistance sought – was like having a new life spread out before me, and the sight of it was glorious.

My father did not go straight home, but wandered awhile through Tlaltelolco. He had stopped and

61

turned to speak to me once more when I smelt smoke. I was not alone; suddenly everyone in the crowded street looked towards the temple.

With no warning and no apparent cause, it was violently ablaze. As we watched, wings of flame rushed from the doors of the sacred shrine that topped the pyramid and flared into the sky. For a moment, I was immobilized with shock, but screams of "Bring water!", "Fill jars!", "Put it out!" and "The temple must not burn!" brought me to my senses.

With so many people dousing the fire – it seemed everyone who heard the cries ran to help – surely the building would be saved? A woman came from her house, a jar under each arm. Taking one from her, I filled it from the canal and ran up the steps, throwing my water on the flames. They only seemed to leap higher in response.

I sped back to the canal. Two, three, four times I scaled those steep steps, and each time the blaze grew stronger. The frantic crowd continued to work, but it was in vain. Although the pyramid streamed with water – my clothes were drenched – the fire would not be put out. At last the throng of people was beaten back by the terrible heat. Stone crumbled like charcoal and with a great crash the temple fell.

Following that heated roar came a deathlike silence broken only by the sound of blood pounding in my ears. I stared at the smoking ruin, sick with fear at what it might mean.

For then the crowd began to whisper of what – or who – had caused the gods such offence that they would strike the shrine in this way. My heart chilled. The deity whose temple now lay in ruins was Tezcatlipoca, the very god whose image I had scratched upon the terracotta tiles of my home.

*T*he fire I had struggled to douse was not the only disaster to befall Tenochtitlán at that time. Some days later, a second temple in the south of the city – that of the god Quetzalcoatl – was struck by a bolt from the sky and burst into flames. I did not see it happen, but word of it spread like a chilling breeze, causing men's brows to furrow and women to whimper softly with fear. There had been no storm, no preceding rumble of thunder, and so it was whispered that the temple had been hit with a blow from the sun. Why the gods should thus turn on each other was a mystery no priest could explain, but there could be no doubt it boded ill.

After that came a day of bright, brilliant sunshine. The sky was clear, the air crisp, with a biting edge that warned of the winter to come. With some determination, I laid aside my own anxiety, telling myself sternly that nothing could happen on a day of such beauty. Taking the honey I had drawn from our rooftop hives, I went alone to the lakeside to barter. Mitotiqui had expressed a desire to eat fresh fish, and I sorely wanted to soothe his ruffled temper.

The fisherman I was used to trading with was in his canoe, some distance from the shore. I would wait for his return. The day was lovely, the lake calm; I welcomed the chance to enjoy a little tranquillity. For too long, it seemed, my heart had been unsettled. Solitude would ease away my troubles.

Sitting myself down beside the lake in the shade of the willows, I watched the fisherman cast his net as if it were a weightless thing. I knew well that it was not. Once – long ago – he had let Mitotiqui and me try the skill for ourselves. Standing on the ground, we had barely been able to lift the complex construction of knotted twine from the earth. If we had attempted such a thing in a canoe we would certainly have toppled overboard. How he had laughed to see us struggling, tangling ourselves in the net like a large catch! I smiled to recall it.

Moments later the fisherman hauled, hand over hand, pulling his net out with ease, the scales of many fish glinting silver in the sun. But as I watched, the distant fish became so dazzling that I had to blink hard, shutting my eyes against their glare. When I opened them, it was no better. The whole lake seemed suddenly ablaze. In the blinding light I could barely trace the fisherman's outline. He stood frozen in his canoe, back bent, head tilted skywards in awe of the spectacle above him.

I looked up, and expelled a sharp cry. I backed away, desperately looking for a place to run, to hide. But where could I run? How could I hide from the sky itself? For above me a ball of fire was tearing across the heavens. Larger than the sun, it lit the world below so brightly that I was seared by its brilliance. It split the sky, ripping it apart and leaving a black wound to mark its passing. Then it fell where the sun rises, trailing a shower of sparks like a hail of red-hot coals.

It took less time to pass than it takes to roll a tortilla. When it was gone, a dreadful quiet remained. I could see no one but myself and the fisherman, but I could feel the sense of horror rising from the city behind me as strong as the heat of summer. After the last spark came to earth it was as though every inhabitant stood mouth open, unable to speak. Then, with one breath, all began to gabble at once. From the edge of the water where I stood, the fearful chatter seemed almost visible, hanging like smoke above the buildings.

The spell was broken.

The fisherman rowed to shore, but when he reached me I saw that his boat was empty. He had lost both catch and net, letting them slip through his fingers as he watched, rigid with terror.

Another incident then occurred which was of longer duration than the ball of fire, and caused much hardship.

After the harvest, when the chinampa fields lay stripped and bare and the maize was dried and stored for winter, a high wind sprang up from a sky that had been perfectly clear and still. In moments it had lashed the lake into a boiling frenzy, stirring up a great wave and driving it towards the city.

I knew nothing of its approach. It was so unexpected, so sudden, that no one had time to give warning. Only when I heard Mayatl's scream of alarm did I turn to see a wall of water surging from the street into our kitchen, picking up reed mats as though they were leaves, sweeping aside cooking vessels, dousing the brazier and pushing it into the courtyard, through my father's chamber and into the workshop beyond. Mayatl stood unmoving, stiff with shock. Wading through the waist-high flood, I seized her hand and pulled her awkwardly up the stairs to the roof. My father – drenched, the necklet he had been working on still clasped in his fist – joined us. From our vantage point we could see that the wave had washed over the fields and destroyed the mud-brick walls of the peasants' dwellings across the canal. While we watched, the water rushed on towards the heart of the city, where my brother would be sitting at his classes.

It was a dreadful sight, but even more dreadful were the words my father then uttered.

"And now it seems Tlaloc is also roused to anger."

"But why?" I whispered. "What can have so displeased him?"

My father did not answer me directly, but spoke aloud the thoughts in his head that filled my own heart with foreboding. "First we had fire; now comes a flood. I fear the earth itself is becoming unmade…"

Deeply alarmed though we were by this incident, our own house was built of stone so it suffered little real damage. Mitotiqui came home from the calmecac in a canoe, bobbing into our courtyard with a smile upon his face as if the episode was nothing more than a prank played by the gods for their own amusement. His levity grated on my father. We were uncomfortable that night, and the nights that followed, for we had to sleep on the roof amongst the beehives and potted herbs. But our physical discomfort seemed small and insignificant beside the tension that crackled between father and son.

Each portent, each strange happening, each untimely occurrence, was answered by our priests with ever greater sacrifices, for the gods were angered and might perhaps be soothed with blood. The numbers of slaves the traders brought to market grew, and they could be seen daily being led through the streets to the principal temple, where their hearts were given up to appease the gods. We were urged to increase our private devotions: priests went about the city punishing those they considered less than pious; and in every household, men drew their own blood before their shrines. My father could be seen each morning at dawn pricking his flesh with cactus thorns and smearing our idols until red almost blotted out the gleaming gold.

These zealous prayers seemed answered. The flood was followed by a time of calm, and yet the general unease continued. Men stood at every street corner gnawing their lips, and passing women stared fearfully at the ground, their faces creased with anxiety. For at heart we all knew that if the fifth age were truly drawing to a close, no amount of prayer or sacrifice could stop it.

In the great square of Tlaltelolco, each incident had been greeted with dismay and fearful speculation.

But one day Mayatl brought home a tale tucked neatly amongst the fresh vegetables to which I could give no credence. Setting her basket down, she declared, "They say floating temples have been seen!"

"Floating temples?" My incredulous gasp gave her great satisfaction. Her eyes gleamed with the delight of knowing something I did not. "How can such a thing be possible? Where were they?"

"On the sea. In the land of the Maya. Great white pyramids, moving across the water."

I related Mayatl's words to my father when he ate, but he grunted scornfully. "Travellers' tales, from men who have eaten too many mushrooms. Pay no heed."

And yet the rumours did not go away, but multiplied until the city swarmed with them. It was impossible to go to market – impossible to venture anywhere – without hearing stories that grew more elaborate with each passing day.

"They say beasts half man, half deer have trodden on the distant shore."

"The Mayans speak of their magical powers."

"They have a great pole that makes a noise as loud as thunder! With one blast it will fell a tree!"

"Destroy a mountain!"

"Wipe out an army!"

Unease soured the air, making each indrawn breath taste bitter on the tongue. I could scarcely believe such far-fetched imaginings, yet my own heart stirred with a strange excitement at hearing these stories. They were so like the inventions that Mitotiqui and I had dreamt up as children, I could not resist their appeal. I relished their tang, as I savoured the spicy heat of chilli, and I repeated them at each mealtime to entertain my family. But my brother was morose and sullen, and my father dismissive.

"Strangers are amongst the Maya," I ventured.

"Strangers?" My father gave a wry laugh. "How could any distinguish a stranger in that land? Who could be more peculiar than a Mayan?"

I smiled briefly at his remark. The Mayans flattened the foreheads of their babies from birth, and hung beads above their cradles so that their eyes grew crossed. Certainly this race looked alien and exotic to the eyes of those from Tenochtitlán.

And yet I persisted. "They say the strangers have pale skin. At the market the talk is of little else."

"Women must always have something to gossip about, Itacate. They pile untruth on untruth until they have made a monster of nothing. There can be no such strangers. It is not possible. Our emperor rules the whole world. Where could they come from? It is folly even to think such a thing could happen."

Thus dismissed, I said no more about the matter. Not to my father. But with Mayatl I talked until my tongue was dry. The tales lingered in my head and I could not be free of them. I put them aside only when my father made a proposal that drove all thoughts of strangers far from my mind.

My father wished me to work alongside him as his apprentice. He was ageing, and though his eyes were well able to view distant objects, he struggled to focus on what was close to his face. The small detail of the objects he crafted had become increasingly blurred and hazy.

There was great danger in yielding to his wish. To step outside our city's conventions could bring misfortune or even death. If a merchant offended the nobility by mimicking their style of dress, he could be condemned to slavery. If a common man drank the intoxicating pulque reserved for priests and nobles, he could be executed. I knew not what penalty might be inflicted on a father who allowed his daughter to aid his work, or on a girl who agreed to help him, but had no doubt that it would be severe.

It was vital that I work in secrecy; I could tell no one. Not Mayatl. Not even Mitotiqui. They must think my father required my company, nothing else.

I had already left off my kitchen tasks, but now the remainder of my domestic duties were passed to a grumbling Mayatl. Daily I crossed the threshold of my father's chamber, passing through it to the rear courtyard, and across that to his workshop. It was a journey of a few short steps, but how far it took me from my old life! My heart joyed to have constant access to a room of such wonders, even as it sorrowed to keep this secret from my brother.

To begin with, my father had simply wished for a helper to grade stones, for he could no longer see the marks and fissures that divided inferior gems from those of higher quality. I found the finest for him, but one morning as I did so could not resist speaking of what it might become.

"Would this not make a fine headdress?" I asked tentatively, holding up a clear and perfect jade.

"Set how?" he said, taking the stone.

"High above the head. So the sun will shine through and illuminate the colour."

His approving grunt gave me greater confidence. Later, on matching turquoise stones of even size and hue, I ventured, "These speak to me of a breastplate,

Father. Would they not look fine arranged in a pattern, thus?"

He nodded at each suggestion I made, and I had the great pleasure of seeing the ideas I provided fashioned by him into marvels of gold. Freed from grinding domesticity, my spirit soared and my mind was unleashed.

It was not long before he moved me on to other tasks: refining beeswax, stoking up the charcoal-heated furnace, setting grains of gold in a vessel to melt. I proved competent, and one afternoon he said softly, "I begin to wonder if the skill in your fingers might match the ideas in your head. I think, perhaps, your talent may exceed my own." He looked at me thoughtfully, plucking at his ear lobe, his eyebrows drawn together. "I feel the temptation, Itacate. Some god dangles possibilities before me. Am I to yield, or reject them?"

He did not expect me to give an answer; he was merely speaking his thoughts aloud. I sat, head bowed, while he considered my future. "I know not if your skill is a gift from the gods, or a means of bringing disaster down upon us." He sighed heavily, and was quiet for some time. But when I lifted my face I saw that he had come to a decision. "I find I cannot resist my own curiosity. I am eager to see what you can do. Let us begin."

And so it was – with trembling hands lest he offend the gods in doing so – my father taught me the skills of the goldsmith. Over the days and months that followed, I learnt first to make small beads which I then strung together onto necklets. Under his supervision, I created lip plugs. Earrings. Breastplates. The time I had spent moulding tortilla dough into models had made my fingers nimble. My work was good, and each day I felt my powers in the art grow.

When my father reasoned that I had learnt enough of his methods, he pressed a lump of beeswax into my palm. In his own hand he held Mitotiqui's ill-crafted necklet.

"It may be unwise to do this; the gods alone know what will come of it. And yet, surely it must be they who have given you this gift? I want to see how you fare with a larger piece. You are to fashion this next work entirely on your own. I am going to unmake this," he said, holding my brother's creation. "You shall have this jade for your figurine."

I did not watch him set the necklet in the fire to melt the gold away from the stone, but I felt a stab of pain on my brother's behalf. His handiwork was wiped out as though it had never been. I was delighted to have the jade, and yet a fissure of sadness ran through my happiness, making it brittle and as likely to be fractured as Popotl's rejected amber.

But I had been given a task. I had to push thoughts of Mitotiqui away while my fingers, so much smaller and more dextrous than my father's, shaped the figurine that I had scratched upon the tile.

I was not satisfied with my first attempt, and balled the wax in my fist before my father saw it. My second was an improvement, although I was not content, for the god's face was dull and lifeless. My father examined my work, and pronounced himself pleased, but I was not.

"I will try once more."

"It is time to eat."

"I will come when I have finished."

I chose not to accompany him to where Mayatl was laying out food on reed mats, but sat instead in the second courtyard of my home reworking the wax effigy in the fading light. I did not stop until sundown, when the image in my hand more closely matched the one I held in my head. I pressed the jade into the god's palm, leaving an imprint where the stone would be set once I had cast the figure in gold, and admired my work with pleasure.

By then it was too dark to cover the figure with clay: I needed good light to ensure I left no holes that might mar the mould and put blemishes upon my statue. I would begin again at dawn. Setting down the waxen effigy I felt a tremor of nervousness: I had scratched the god's image, and a temple had burnt. Would anything follow the making of this idol? I pushed the thought aside. I was a small, insignificant creature. Was I not beneath the notice of the gods?

That night I dreamt of my mother.

In life I had never seen her face, for she had been buried before I had even been given my bathing ceremony. But in this dream world I saw her, smiling, reaching out a hand to draw me lovingly towards her, her features the mirror of my own.

I took my mother's hand and yielded to her embrace, feeling the warm glow of happy contentment. But the tranquillity of this dream was suddenly shattered when I felt her tears on my neck. Her words when they came were not soft endearments, but mournful cries.

"We must flee the city!"

I looked at her in wonder, but could frame no reply. In my dream I had no voice. As I watched, my mother opened her mouth once more, but this time I realized the words had not come from her but from some far distant place. Dreadful shrieks of lamentation drowned what my mother was trying to tell me.

A woman was screaming, "My children, we must make haste. Where can I take you?" I bent my ear to my mother's lips, but she dissolved and vanished as I woke.

It was then I realized the cries that had penetrated my dream came from outside the house. I heard the woman's voice again.

"Children! We must go far away! You must run! Flee now, before it is too late!"

The sound made me quiver with fear but I stood and, taking a cloak to ward off the night chill, prepared to go from the chamber that I still shared with Mayatl. She was in a deep slumber, unlikely to stir. Mitotiqui had long since moved into my father's bedchamber, and I turned towards it, intending to rouse him. But then the glow of charcoal and the movement of a shadow in the kitchen caught my attention and I changed direction.

The night was dark, the moon obscured by thick cloud, but Mitotiqui was there before me, heaping embers from the brazier into a vessel that we might have a little light. In their glow I saw puzzlement line his face. Who could be disturbing the peace of the night with such dreadful screams? Without a word, we went together to discover the cause.

We found no one. We passed into the street, where many of our neighbours stood, likewise roused, huddled in groups, uncertain of what to do. It was instinct to offer comfort to the woman whose weeping rent the air. But though we could hear her cries quite clearly and distinctly, we could see no one that gave them voice.

The sounds began to move away, as if the woman was walking towards the marketplace. Fretfully wringing their hands, our neighbours returned to their dwellings, but Mitotiqui and I followed the noise through the streets and alleys, across the market square, which stood strangely still and empty in the dead of night. We followed until we came to the very edge of the city, and nothing was before us but the ink-black lake.

We stood gazing out across the water.

"Perhaps we missed her in the dark," said Mitotiqui uncertainly.

"Perhaps," I replied. For it was more pleasant to think we had failed than that the cries had some unnatural cause.

It was not the cold night air that made us shiver, but a sigh of lament behind us, so heavy that we felt the breath of it on our necks. We turned, expecting at last to find her.

We saw nothing.

The cries began again – so near that it sounded as though the woman stood between us. But Mitotiqui and I were utterly alone. And then she moved on, gliding impossibly across the water, her voice fading as she drifted far away towards the eastern shore.

We could not then doubt that this was a sign sent by the gods: a warning of some great evil to come. And there beside the lake, my brother and I clung to each other for support, as we had done when we were children.

My father had slept through the wailing that had roused Mitotiqui and me from our slumbers. But the streets were awash with anxious mutterings, and by the time we returned to our house they had inevitably reached his ears. He sat in the kitchen with Mayatl, cupping a vessel of warm broth in his hands that seemed more for comfort than nourishment, for he did not drink it.

"It signals something," he muttered. "We have offended the gods."

He looked at me and his eyes pierced mine. I knew his meaning. As soon as day dawned he would banish me from his workshop. I felt the pressure of the loom on my back; saw the threads stretching before me. I could not return to that entrapment!

At that moment, I saw that I was no longer the discarded, dried-out husk I had once considered myself to be. As my skill had grown, so had my heart, my soul. I had become entire and whole, and as distinct and separate as my brother. I could not now lose myself!

Feeling Mitotiqui's gaze upon me, I chose my words carefully. "It cannot be so, Father," I said. "Surely no one in our city has caused this omen. There is some greater reason. Perhaps the gods warn us of the strangers who are amongst the Maya."

"Perhaps," he conceded, shivering. But he would not meet my eyes.

We returned to our beds and spoke of the unseen woman no more.

Despite my father's misgivings, I finished the figurine. I was eloquent in my pleading, and at last he yielded to my persuasion. Some compulsion drove me forward, and, believing it was the hand of fate, I convinced myself that I was powerless against it. But in reality it was my own stubbornness that steered me – the same stubbornness that had made me live, despite Pachtic's conviction that I was stillborn. The stubbornness that set my will against that of the gods.

The stubbornness that would lead me to disaster.

When my father judged we had made sufficient goods, we took them to market. He summoned a boatman for the purpose; though the distance was short we did not want to carry items of such value openly through the streets.

We left before sunrise, climbing into the canoe as girls carrying baskets of warm tortillas sped towards temples to take food to the priests. My figurine was amongst the gold and silverware piled high in several baskets and covered with cloths. These were set carefully in the middle of the vessel. My father sat at the head, and I at the rear, beside the boatman. I was to accompany him as a helper – a fetcher and carrier. At all times I had to keep my eyes cast down. No one should suspect I was anything more than an assistant, brought to help him with the most menial of tasks.

We reached the busy canal as dawn broke and the conch blasts rang forth. Here we joined the jostle of canoes that sought space to tie up and unload their cargoes. A steward of the council directed our boatman to a clear stretch where a porter waited, and here we disembarked. Once we were ashore, the same steward briefly inspected our wares and allotted a pitch where we might sell them.

It was near to that of Popotl, who greeted my father warmly, like an old friend. "Oquitchli! I have fine gems for you today. Obsidian as black as Mictlan; emeralds as green as a quetzal's feathers; turquoises as blue as the spring sky."

"I am sure they are all fine stones," replied my father. "But today, Popotl, we have come to sell."

My eyes were lowered, as they should be, but I heard an intrigued note in Popotl's voice. *"We?"* he asked.

He had barely set foot in the square and already my father had made an error. I was nothing – a girl – and should not have been included in his plans. But the words were out; my father could not recall them.

"We," he repeated with a casual laugh. "My daughter is with me, as you see. She is required, sometimes, to fetch and carry. She is cheaper than a slave," he joked loudly, adding in an undertone for my ears only: "Cheaper, but perhaps more trouble."

Popotl grunted. He made no other remark, but I knew I must behave as the perfect, humble, invisible daughter if I were not to inflame his curiosity further.

It was an agonizing task. As wealthy men began to arrive in the square and peruse the goods we had laid upon the reed mats, I was desperate to see if my work was appreciated; if any noticed its quality. But instead I had to kneel on the ground behind my father, fix my eyes on a corner of the mat and never look up, not once.

I could not watch their faces and had to imagine

the rest of their bodies from what I could see of their feet. One man – of great antiquity it seemed to me – came with feet so withered that the bones were almost visible through the flesh. His nails overhung the ends of his toes, curving like the claws of a jaguar. A crabbed hand reached down and took the figurine I had so carefully crafted. What great temptation it was to look up and see his expression! But I resisted, keeping my eyes fixed on those hideous feet. And when he threw my work back down – dropping it with an icy grunt of contempt – I managed not to move, not to stir, not to cry out with the offended pride of a craftsman. I stiffened, but that was all, and even as I did so I hoped desperately that Popotl had not noticed; I felt in some obscure way that the trader was a threat to me.

By mid morning my father had sold much, exchanging lip plugs and necklets for cloaks, or the gold-filled quills and cocoa beans that were currency for goods as valuable as ours. As the sun reached its zenith and my body ached with immobility, a nobleman stopped before us.

I discerned his high status at once. Many in the city go barefoot or wear simple sandals, but this man wore shoes of finely tooled leather. His smooth skin gleamed with scented oil, and the cape that hung to his ankles was brightly coloured, woven in the

85

finest of threads and edged with dazzling feathers of immense cost. I could hear the tinkling of the golden bells that adorned his person; members of the nobility like to be heard as well as seen. This man was clearly one of the elite.

I felt his shadow upon me as he bent to pick something from our display of wares. My figurine! I held myself still only with great effort; my body tensed with the strain of it.

The nobleman spoke. "You are a merchant?"

"No, my lord," said my father, his tone slightly muffled as though his head was bowed in a gesture of respect. "I am a craftsman."

"You fashioned this?"

My father, a truthful man, hesitated. "It was made in my workshop, my lord."

"It is fine work. Remarkably fine. I took it to be Mixtec."

"Thank you, my lord."

The compliment was great indeed. Our goldsmiths had long ago learnt their art from the Mixtec race, and many still rated their work superior to our own.

The nobleman agreed a price with my father – a high one – and made to leave with the figurine. But before he departed he asked, "Your name?"

"Oquitchli."

"Oquitchli," he repeated as if to fix it in his mind. "You dwell in Azcapotzalco?"

"No, my lord," replied my father. "Here, in the Tlaltelolco district."

"Indeed?" The nobleman was greatly surprised that my father did not live in the goldsmiths' region. "I may have a commission for you. Where can I find you?"

My father did not give directions to our house. Instead he said, "If you wish it, my lord, I shall be here next market day."

"I do." The nobleman turned and departed.

My father made no comment. He could not. We had to make a pretence of mutual indifference. He talked instead with Popotl: idle chatter concerning the gossip of the market and the court.

As the trading day drew to a close, and we packed our few unsold wares back into the reed baskets, I felt the assessing eyes of Popotl heavy upon me.

Not until we were safely back in his workshop did my father speak of what had happened, and then his words were muted. "Well, Itacate. It seems you may bring wealth to your family. And attention."

He said no more, and I did not reply. Instead I went to help Mayatl prepare the meal, dull labour soothing my fevered thoughts.

As I peeled avocado and set slices in an earthen-ware bowl, I considered the whereabouts of our

87

home. It stood alone, several streets away from the marketplace, between the mud-brick huts of the peasant farmers and the larger stone-built dwellings of the potters' guild. My father had always lived quietly – avoiding contact with others, producing wares that were competently crafted but unremarkable. I had believed he did so because he cared little for his life. But now I detected the reasoning that lay behind his choice. As a goldsmith, he was exempt from paying taxes and thus, until that moment, we had been beneath the notice of the authorities. But now my figurine had brought my father – and his defiance of the conventions of our city – to the attention of one of the elite.

I trembled at the thought of what my father's curiosity and my stubbornness might cost us.

*B*etween that market day and
the next came the spring festival which honoured
the god Tezcatlipoca: four days of ritual that made
the heart ache with sadness even as it sang with
joy, for it celebrated the frailty of love, the fleeting-
ness of beauty, the fragility of fame and grandeur.
The ill omens of the past months gave the festival a
desperate, ardent intensity, for it was through the
favour of Tezcatlipoca that our empire had been
created; by his grace that Montezuma sat aloft
as lord of the world. But all knew that the god
who had made Tenochtitlán great could as easily
destroy it.

As was the custom a handsome youth – unblem-
ished and perfect – had been chosen to represent the
deity, and for the whole of the past sacred year he

had lived removed from the world as though divine. At the start of the festival he would be given four handmaidens – great beauties of the elite – who would share his life and warm his bed on his last days on earth. Carried about the city in a litter, he would have flowers strewn in his path and his glory would match that of the emperor himself. All would bow reverentially before him, and some would kiss the ground and implore him to intercede with the gods on their behalf.

And on the fourth day, at the very peak of the celebrations, this splendid youth would mount the steps of the principal temple. Breaking the flute that tied him to this world, he would then gladly submit himself for sacrifice. Thus, we hoped, would Tezcatlipoca's favour be bought for one more year. Thus, we hoped, would Tenochtitlán's great fame and bountiful good fortune continue.

Before then there were three days of feasting and dancing.

For many months now it had seemed as though Mitotiqui and I stood on either side of a broad canal and someone had smashed the bridge between us. He no longer told me about his days at school, and I could tell him nothing of my growing mastery of the goldsmith's art. When he was released from the calmecac, he did not hurry home to seek my company as he used to, but disappeared with other young men, doing I knew not what.

But the first day of the festival was different. It was a holy time and the priests who taught him were engaged with other duties so he had no school. And I, our father complaining of a headache, was released from my work. Mayatl was occupied with the many tasks of the household. So Mitotiqui and I went together to the temple precinct to watch the celebrations.

Our mood was muted at first; we hardly knew how to speak to one another. We walked the wide avenues, and the distance between us was tangible and painfully awkward. But as we continued the crowds became thicker, until they were so great that we were pressed shoulder to shoulder. This enforced contact began to dissolve our reticence.

Like all gods, Tezcatlipoca has two faces: one is perfect and beautiful; the other is Titlacuan the destroyer, a wizened old man full of malice. This duality was represented throughout the festival. As Mitotiqui and I approached the square, a shrunken, aged man, whose curled toenails clacked on the stones like claws, leapt in our path and waved his stick in our faces. By his feet I knew him to be the man from the marketplace – he who had cast down my figurine in scorn. His eyes blazed as the god possessed him. Stepping forward to shield me, Mitotiqui took the blows Titlacuan rained down. They thudded hard upon his chest, while he who played the god shrieked aloud, "Do not protect her! She brings disaster."

It was his usual cry. He moved on, poking his stick rudely beneath the skirts of women, and shouting insults to their husbands. But it chilled me; his words seemed meant for my ears alone. Seeing my reaction, Mitotiqui placed an arm about my shoulders and pulled me to him.

"Come, sister," he said. "The bird dance begins."

As children, we had always thought this the most exciting aspect of the festival.

A high pole had been erected in the precinct and four men, dressed in the costumes of birds with intricate weavings of gold and green feathers transforming their arms into wings, climbed it. When they reached the platform at the top they tied ropes around their waists. A fifth man was perched perilously at the centre, a drum gripped between his knees which he began to beat.

Once secured, with no hesitation the first of the four dived off, head first, hurtling towards the ground. I knew he was safely secured, knew he would not dash himself to pieces; yet I, along with the rest of the onlookers, could not help but gasp as he launched himself into the air. He scarce brushed the stone before springing back up. Around the pole he bobbed and spun, wheeling in a great arc high above our heads thirteen times – a sacred number, for it is as many as the cycle of years, and the layers of the heavens.

The second and third bird dancers followed the first almost at once. But the fourth was slow to dive, as though afraid. And when the jeers of the crowd forced him off, he found he had misjudged the length of his rope and his head hit stone. We did not hear the crack of bone, for the watching people roared, some with sympathy, some with derision. His flight was erratic, inelegant, of no tribute to the gods. When it ended he was led, almost insensible, away.

"I fear for him," murmured my brother in my ear.

"I too."

We both knew that an error in any dance could prove fatal to the perpetrator.

Next came the nobles of the city, hundreds of men wearing gorgeous robes of rippling feathers, gleaming with gold ornaments. Drums sounded, and the music of pipes and flutes rang throughout the square. The noblemen began the serpent dance, rising in waves in tribute to Tezcatlipoca. The assembled crowd clapped and whooped, giving their encouragement and support to those who wound, with wild ecstasy, in spiralling circles around the drummers. Attendants with pine cudgels stood ready to press back any man who weakened and tried to leave the dance. The steps must be performed correctly until the very end; any deviation from the pattern was an offence. This dance was done not for idle pleasure or amusement; this was an act of worship that demanded the total dedication of the participant's body, mind and soul.

When it was over Mitotiqui grasped my hand. I turned to him, and suddenly we were children again – giggling infants who had escaped the clutches of our nurse. We abandoned the festivities and fled, winding between streets and alleyways, heading for the chinampa fields.

So absorbed were we in our reckless flight that we almost ran headlong into the procession. Only when the priests nearly stepped upon us did we realize our danger. We swiftly stood aside, flattening ourselves against a wall, heads bowed low in respect, wiping all traces of amusement from our faces.

It was the god. The perfect youth was carried upon a litter, garlanded and magnificently clothed. I knelt as he passed, as was the custom; but as I did so, some impulse spurred me to glance at him.

For a moment, I was blinded by beauty – stunned

by the radiance of his face. Glory scalded the backs of my eyes. This was no mortal boy. He was transformed, possessed by the god, lit from within by his power. The youth he had been was burnt away, and what remained of his body was a gilded shell: unreal, insubstantial, a dream. And soon the door would open to a more lasting truth – the eternal reality. I closed my eyes to shut out the brightness of his divinity, pressing my palms hard against the lids.

The procession of priests and handmaidens to the god moved on, and Mitotiqui and I were left alone once more. I could breathe again, and did so, inhaling in fevered gulps. Our rash act had brought us close to incurring the wrath of the priests and it would be death to do so.

My brother did not notice my distress.

"Look," he said, his voice quivering with excitement as he held out his open palm for inspection. "See what the god has left us."

It was not the food of commoners; not a thing that could be freely purchased in the market square. But I had often seen girls carrying baskets towards the temples; I knew at once what they were.

Mushrooms. Five of them. The sacred diet of priests and gods. They had rolled from the litter of the perfect youth and been found by my own perfect brother. He pressed two into my hand.

"These are for you. I will have three," he decided.

"Because you are a man?" I asked, my temper rising in irritation.

"No, dear sister, because I am bigger. I need more food. You know my appetite has always been greater than yours." So saying he crammed the mushrooms into his mouth and chewed.

How could I do anything but copy him? He was my beloved brother, and for too long I had ached with his absence. Where he led, I would follow.

I started to eat.

For some time we simply stood and stared at each other, feeling a little stupid. I had expected the effect to be instantaneous, and it was not.

But then – like a rising mist – the mushrooms began their work.

I cannot describe all that happened next, because I do not recall it. I know that I had a sensation of floating above the streets and over the roofs. I yearned to soar high into the sky, to see at last what lay beyond the mountains. And yet I was prevented by a great weight that tethered me to the ground. Looking down, I recognized this as my own body, which was slumped beside Mitotiqui in the street. From above I watched as he pulled me to my feet and, with an arm about my waist, walked with me back towards the temple precinct. His steps were uneven, his gait strange and stumbling, as though he too would soon collapse. Drugged as I was, I felt it unwise to be amongst crowds where our condition would be observed. I wanted to tell him to go in a different direction, but in my spirit-like state I had lost the power of speech.

A hazy blur of dancers whirled about the square, and the drums grew louder and louder. I saw Mitotiqui fall, insensible, at the steps of the temple, my empty body lying discarded beside him. I was caught up, spinning out of control, insubstantial as a breeze, blowing hither and thither amongst the whirling dancers until suddenly everything ceased.

The last thing I saw clearly was the face of a man – a strange youth I had never met – whose golden hair grew in waving lines like the plumed serpents of the god Quetzalcoatl. After that, everything was darkness and silence.

It was many hours later that I revived. The crowds had thinned as the festivities were over for that day. The sun was almost set.

It was our father who found us. Our father who, becoming anxious at our absence, had set forth to search the city for his children. His was the face before me when I opened my eyes.

But it was not his voice that said coldly, "You ate of the mushroom."

It was not a question.

A priest. Painted black for the festival. Matted hair thick with blood. Ears torn with lacerations. Eyes blazing as he asked, "What did you see?"

My mouth seemed full of ash. Words were difficult. I whispered, "A man – a youth. That was all."

"Your future husband, perhaps," said my father lightly. "Is that not all girls ever dream of?" His tone was mocking, as if to convey that my actions had been merely foolish, not blasphemous.

I did not correct him. I did not dare to say that the youth I had seen was like no one who walked in this world. Hearing the fear in my father's voice, I held my tongue.

"Come, my daughter." He helped me to my feet. "Let us go home. I had need of you today."

But the priest had not finished with us. He looked at Mitotiqui, who, like me, had only just awoken from his vision, and who now stared with jealousy at the protective hand our father had placed on my shoulder. Our father had made no move to help him. Terror kept him still. I felt his fingers tremble as they gripped me, but Mitotiqui could not see this.

"You, boy," asked the priest. "You ate too?"

"Youthful folly," my father said swiftly. "An accident, no more."

"Nothing happens by accident," the priest snapped

in reply. He turned to my brother. "What did the gods show you?"

Did Mitotiqui know where his words would lead him? Did he speak the truth? I tortured myself with those questions in the months that followed, but could not find the answer.

Certainly I had not realized the depths of my brother's hurt until then; had not known how desperate his desire for our father's attention. I saw impetuous words rising in him, and longed to clap my hand upon his mouth to stop them spilling forth. But before I could move he had spoken.

Mitotiqui's eyes met our father's. It was to him Mitotiqui looked when he answered the priest.

"I saw the face of the god. Today I have walked beside Tezcatlipoca."

"You are certain?"

My brother nodded. "I am."

The priest fell upon him, and as if from nowhere a dozen more appeared, surrounding my brother like vultures clustering around a corpse. One daubed his cheeks with blue pigment and gave a triumphant shout.

"Tezcatlipoca!"

The cry was taken up by the others, and the air rang with their shrill voices. I felt hollow as a drum. My chest, my stomach and my bowels reverberated with the priests' ecstatic yells as my brother was taken from me.

Three days later, the beautiful youth we had seen in the procession mounted the temple steps, broke his flute and submitted himself to the priests. Horns sounded as his beating heart was torn from his chest. Moments later, the flute of the new Tezcatlipoca was heard across the city.

I could not join in the rejoicing, could feel nothing but a wild, panicked desolation; for the beautiful, perfect youth chosen as replacement – he who would live the life of a god until next year's sacrifice – was Mitotiqui.

On the day that followed, we moved as if in a dream. My father and I left for market with a single basket of goods to sell. We would not usually have gone with so little, but my father had promised the nobleman he could be found there, and felt it unwise to displease him.

We spoke little of Mitotiqui. He had been led away by the bloodied, stinking priests to be dressed in the vestments of Tezcatlipoca. Even as we were rowed to market, he would be dining on the finest food, waited on by a myriad of slaves, living a life of idleness and pleasure. He had become the god. I would see him no more; he was already dead to me. And for this, I was supposed to feel joyful.

My father had said only, "At his birth a splendid future was foretold for him. It seems the priests were right. There could be no greater glory."

It was the correct – the proper – thing to say, but I knew not whether my father's heart was in the words. He too had seen the look upon Mitotiqui's face: did it now torment him as it did me?

Amongst the young men of the city, there was great rivalry to be chosen to play the part Mitotiqui had now won. Maybe he had talked of it with his schoolfellows. Maybe he had desired it. I should have been content. Yet I could not rid myself of the fear that my brother's act had been born of jealousy. His words had come unthinkingly. And what a price he would pay for his impulsiveness, not only now but for all eternity! Tezcatlipoca must have a willing sacrifice. If my brother's life was not joyfully given, he would not enter paradise. If he shamed the god, he would enter the perpetual night of Mictlan.

I dared not speak of my concerns, for if Tezcatlipoca heard me it would provoke his anger. But in my heart I raged against the gods. I had never before doubted or questioned them, and yet I did so now. Blasphemously, heretically, I stormed against their weakness – berating them for their fragility that they must have blood to make the sun rise, the seasons turn, the maize grow. Why were they not strong enough to do these things unaided? Why must Tezcatlipoca's favour be bought at so high a price? Why must he have the living heart of my brother?

I had to keep my face composed; no one could know the turmoil within me. I remembered too well what had happened to the mother of a boy taken as sacrifice to Tlaloc, the water god. During the ceremony she had wept – as did we all – for the more tears that flow, the greater the devotion shown to he who makes the rain fall. But then she had begun to wail without restraint, pleading, begging the priests to let her son live. She had leapt forward and attempted to stay the priest's hand.

She had been chastised. Painful death and eternal night were her punishment.

I could not bemoan Mitotiqui's fate. I had to hold my tongue. Bite it, though it bled, to keep it still.

My father and I were subdued when we arrived at the marketplace. It was easy for me to keep my eyes lowered, but to move with restraint and then keep still upon the reed mat was harder. My heart was heavy, and yet my limbs ached for activity as if by moving they could relieve its dreadful weight.

Word of Mitotiqui's elevation to deity spread quickly from trader to trader, and thus we had to endure the congratulations of every passer-by. The old man with jaguar-clawed feet croaked his delight loudly into the ears of my father.

Popotl had not returned to his home in Cholula but remained in Tenochtitlán to enjoy the festival. Now he came over to us, loud and hearty, and slapped my father upon the back. "And so you have a god in the family, Oquitchli! How much higher can your fortunes rise?"

From the corner of my eye I saw finely tooled shoes weaving between the bare feet of the populace. The nobleman approached.

"We shall see," my father answered briefly; and Popotl, noticing the elite one coming closer, hurried away to array his own goods to their best advantage.

This time the nobleman did not gaze at the goods spread out at his leisure. He was swift in his dealings with my father. I could not hear their conversation above the noise of the crowd, so softly was it spoken. The nobleman was gone in but a few moments. And then my father bent low to address me.

"Pack our goods, Itacate. We must go."

His voice was urgent, his tone anxious. I did as he asked without question and, ignoring the raised eyebrows and curious expressions of the other traders, we left the market.

Huddled at the far end of the canoe where the boatman could not hear us, my father told me what had been said.

"It seems your figurine has attracted great praise. The emperor himself has admired it."

He looked as brittle as a beetle whose wing cases have been ripped off. I opened my mouth but said nothing. My actions had exposed him to the attention of great ones and I was full aware of his fear. And yet delight sprang within me to know my work was valued. I – who could do nothing, hope for nothing – had made a piece that was valued by Montezuma, lord and ruler of the world! It would live here on earth while I wandered the gloomy darkness of Mictlan. The knowledge would light my path. There was some small satisfaction in that.

I thought he had finished, but there was more to come. Rubbing his forehead to hold back the ache that grew there, my father added, "We are to go to the palace. Now. In haste. And in secrecy. We are to tell no one – *no one* – of this. He was most insistent on that point."

"I am to come too, Father?"

"Yes. We have not the time to return home. Besides, the emperor has said he wishes the artist who crafted the figurine to come to him. In all conscience I cannot go without you."

"But I am a girl," I protested. "I cannot be introduced to the emperor! Are you to lose both your children?"

My father's hand squeezed mine in reassurance. "I will not tell him you fashioned it, Itacate. It would be death to do so. But I need your eyes, your ears, your judgement on what is said. The nobleman knows we come straight from the market. He will understand I could not leave you or my wares behind. You will be my carrier. You are a woman. Behave like one. Be invisible."

The boatman had brought us to the canal that edged the great temple precinct. We disembarked and turned to face the palace of Emperor Montezuma.

We were expected. Eagerly awaited. That much became obvious as soon as we approached. We were uncertain of where to enter the vast labyrinth of courtyards and corridors that lay before us, but as we hesitated the nobleman himself came out to meet us. I need not have been afraid of accompanying my father. So insignificant was I that the nobleman did not even glance in my direction. Instead, he ushered my father swiftly into the palace, and I was left to scurry along behind, small and worthless as an insect.

"My name is Axcahuah," the nobleman informed my father. "I am adviser to our lord emperor. I will take you to him now. Keep close behind me."

When I beheld the interior, I felt as though my

breath had been punched from my chest. If I were to die – if the emperor discovered my impudence and punished me for it – I could not help but feel the glory of the palace made the risk worthwhile.

I had to lower my eyes and be silent. And yet I could not keep myself from darting looks here and there; and each time my gaze fell upon some new wonder, it almost stopped me in my tracks. It was not simply the lavish scale of the building, nor the astounding wealth of our emperor, but the exquisite quality of the craftsmanship that was all about me.

I had often heard my father quote the poem: "The good artist is wise; the gods are in his heart." But I had never seen the divine force that inspires and guides all artists' work so powerfully manifested. The many stone pillars that held up the roof were intricately carved with depictions of the gods, and their complex detail made my mind spin. I could do little more than glimpse each one as we passed, and yet I saw a spiritual, sacred depth to the craftsmanship which drew my breath from me. I could spend a lifetime studying these columns and not learn all!

We were led through a series of interlocking courtyards: some cool and leafy, where exotic waterfowl swam on deep ponds and the air was scented with blossom and sweet incense; some sunny and bright, where acrobats, jugglers and musicians practised their skills. We passed an aviary, where colourful birds filled the palace with their trilling song; a menagerie where panthers paced and coyotes howled.

As we neared the centre of the palace I had to bite my lip to stop myself from crying out in delight.

We were approaching a set of broad steps that led upwards to another floor, which in itself was a curiosity to me, for only the royal palace was permitted to have two levels. The steps were dappled with light as the sun broke through the leafy vegetation of two tall trees that stood either side. But the shadows were unmoving, for theirs was not the living foliage of real shrubs. The trunks were silver; the leaves beaten gold; the twig tips dotted with cunningly crafted turquoise flowers. Silver monkeys dangled in their branches; and beneath, two golden jaguars lay, their emerald eyes glinting.

Axcahuah, who was familiar with the sight, did not even pause, but my father broke his step, stopping and reaching out a hand as if he could not believe what his eyes beheld. My own jaw fell open, and no exertion of will could close it. Sharp words from the nobleman recalled us both to our senses, and we began to climb the steps.

Above, we passed through several chambers whose walls were decorated with vivid murals of expert skill. Each room was of such a vast size that the whole of our own house could have fitted easily within.

At last Axcahuah stopped. "This is the throne room," he said quietly.

We had come to a place whose grandeur exceeded all I had yet seen. Though a golden, richly feathered screen stood in the doorway, it could not conceal the lofty height of the chamber, nor the lavish splendour of the painted walls. Gilded images of the gods adorned every surface.

My throat tightened. Saliva flooded my mouth but I strained to swallow. From the sinews that rose like reeds in my father's neck, I knew he was as fearful as I at what was to come.

From behind the screen many slaves came forth, and at once we were sprinkled with sweet incense lest we offend the emperor's nostrils. At the nobleman's instruction we fell to our knees, arms stretched out before us, foreheads pressed to the floor in reverence. The screen was drawn aside, and one by one we crawled into the throne room.

It was a difficult task to edge forward. The basket of goods I pushed before me blocked the sight I had of my father's heels, and in panic I wondered how I should know when to stop moving. I could neither see nor hear him, for so many slaves rushed hither and thither that their footfalls covered all other sounds.

The room was long, and we moved so slowly our passage across the floor seemed to take an eternity. But eventually Axcahuah halted my advance by speaking.

"My lord emperor," said the nobleman. "If it pleases your magnificence, this is the craftsman you commanded me to bring you."

When the emperor spoke, he did so with great gentleness; he had no need to raise his voice. As soon as his lips parted, the air became hushed, taut with expectation.

"I thank you, Axcahuah." He addressed my father. "Goldsmith. Come here to me."

I heard my father shuffling forward on his knees.

Our emperor's voice was rich and melodious but the threat in his next words chilled my blood.

"I have summoned you here to make certain objects," he continued. "But take care that you do not reveal this to anyone: if you do, it will mean death, and not only for you. It will mean the ruin of your house to its foundations, the loss of your goods, and the slaughter of all your kinsmen. If you once displease me, all trace of you and your family shall be removed from the earth."

At that moment I was glad to be kneeling, for I

was suddenly faint and dizzy with dread. I trembled at the power of one who could make such threats and, with the lifting of one little finger, give the command that would wipe us away as though we had never existed! And yet I held tight to the knowledge that he valued my statue. Whatever the emperor wanted, I could produce it. In the peace of our own home, I could work without fear.

But our lord emperor had not yet finished. His next sentence fell like an axe blow. He stepped down from the dais and walked closer to my father. I could see his feet! Sandals of such astounding craftsmanship. And his toenails were gilded alternately with gold and silver!

Softly, so that no slave could overhear, he said, "You will make two statues. Of the same quality as the figurine, but much larger. One of the god Tezcatlipoca. And one of the god Quetzalcoatl. You are to make these objects here in my presence so that your work remains secret."

My father's answer came tight and dry. "It shall be done, my lord emperor."

With those few words, our audience was finished. We could not turn our backs on the emperor, and so – shuffling in awkward retreat, dragging my basket with me – we started the long, slow reverse out of the chamber.

I had not gone far when my eye was caught by a tiny movement near the emperor's foot. At the very edge of my vision I saw that something had dropped from him. For a moment, I thought it was a bright jewel, but when it hit the floor it made no sound.

With great shock, I realized that what had fallen was a tear. There – in the centre of his palace, the centre of our city, the centre of the world – Montezuma, our lord emperor, the master of all, was weeping.

11

Axcahuah led us through the corridors to a set of rooms at the rear of the palace.

I was relieved to discover that when the emperor had bid us work in his presence he meant only that we should remain within the palace walls. And although I was sure his power could be felt in each one of those three hundred rooms, we were not to be overseen by him.

The workshops Axcahuah took us to were in the slaves' quarters, apartments that were nonetheless so luxurious they made our own home seem plain as a peasant's hut. Screens shielded the rooms from the view of anyone passing, and I breathed a sigh of relief: perhaps I might aid my father after all.

Yet when we squeezed behind the screens my heart sank to see two other goldsmiths already there.

One was hard at work making a splendid fan, beating a thin sheet of gold into a carved wooden mould that gave an ornate pattern to what would become the fan's centrepiece. Next to him a pile of exquisite feathers showed how it would be trimmed. Another had taken emeralds, setting them into an extraordinary medallion that hung from heavy chains.

Baskets were heaped with gold ready for our use; I had never seen so much in one place. I was used to working with the small grains that were stored in the hollow quills of feathers and traded at market, but here were piled nuggets the size of pebbles! Ten, twenty baskets full of them! Beside these were several vessels containing fine gems. Perfect jade, polished obsidian, a profusion of emeralds, ambers the size of my fist. I could tell at once that these had been brought directly to the palace: stones of this quality never appeared in the marketplace.

The full peril of our situation struck me. I could do nothing before these men. My father would have to create the statues alone; with his failing eyesight he would have to mimic my piece. And if his craftsmanship fell short of the required standard, we would die.

Axcahuah spoke. "This is where you will work. In all haste you must do what our emperor has ordered."

My father nodded. And then he began to lie.

"My lord Axcahuah," he whispered, "I am as anxious as you to do the emperor's bidding. But did he not say I must work in private?"

"These craftsmen too work to the emperor's commission."

"Indeed. But I prefer to follow his command *exactly* as he spoke it. Besides, I have my own trade secrets that I wish to preserve. Techniques that I alone have developed. My methods are unique to me. I would not wish to hand them to a competitor."

Axcahuah raised an eyebrow at my father's impertinence but could not deny his request. He called for slaves and sent them running in search of further screens and drapes. Before long an area that comprised a covered workshop and open courtyard was marked off for my father's personal use.

Into this were then stacked the gold and gems. At the noble's command a charcoal burner, amounts of wax and clay, and the tools for moulding them were brought forth. Sleeping mats and a spread of delicious titbits completed our provisions; we were well supplied and could work undisturbed.

"You can see your daughter safely home before you begin," said Axcahuah.

"If it pleases you, my lord," replied my father hastily, "I should prefer to keep her here. I may need certain tools from my home, and she will be able to fetch them with all due discretion. The emperor commands secrecy and I would not wish to trust anyone else."

"Very well." The nobleman took a last look around our improvised workspace. "You have everything you need?"

I hoped Axcahuah would not notice the irony that tinged my father's voice as he looked at me and answered, "Yes indeed, my lord. Now I have everything."

Like every Aztec emperor who had preceded him, Montezuma made a great display of his wealth. He gave splendid gifts of such high value that no recipient could ever hope to return their worth. This was the mark of his vast power, his huge might, his inestimable riches. My father and I were thus both sensible of the strangeness of being asked to work in a clandestine manner, but dared not discuss it. Instead we began our task.

Our lord had requested a larger copy of my figurine and so we started with this. Picking through the gems, I selected those that would adorn my statues. I found a disc of obsidian, black and so highly polished that I could see my face in it. It was perfect for Tezcatlipoca, the god of the smoking

116

mirror, old man and perfect youth. He could grant wealth, heroism, nobility, honour. But he was also a capricious trickster, a god of affliction and anguish.

I would make a two-faced figure, then. On one side his visage would be aged and malign, his body as withered as he who had struck my brother's chest at the spring festival. On the reverse he would be splendidly handsome. As handsome as Mitotiqui. I would craft my brother's image in glorious tribute to him. His face, at least, would remain here on earth when his spirit had left for paradise. The obsidian I would set in his hand as the mirror in which Tezcatlipoca viewed the future.

Assessing the quantity of gold we had been supplied with, it became clear that the new figure would have to be made with a hollow core; it could not be solid throughout like the original. In low whispers we debated the wisdom of this.

"Should we request more gold?" I asked. "Will the emperor be displeased if it is not solid like the other?"

"I think we have made trouble enough already. Let us begin, Itacate, and hope that the gods are with us."

The gods. They had stripped me of my brother and now put me and my father in mortal danger. But no... I could not blame them for this situation.

This was my own doing. And with my own hands I could, I hoped, undo it.

Mixing charcoal with clay, I began to create the core of the statue. The emperor had said he wanted it larger than the original, but had not specified a precise size. I would be extravagant: if this was to be my last earthly task, I would make certain the object I created was unforgettable.

My father kept watch. He sat and listened to the sounds of the palace, alert for any who might approach. I was grateful for the nobles' habit of wearing bells upon their cloaks, for they could not come upon us unawares. But slaves move quietly. So do craftsmen. My father was stiff with attention while I worked.

When I had finished the rough shape of the statue that was its core, I set it aside in the sun to harden. I could do nothing more to it until it was firm enough to take the wax I would mould upon its surface to create the detail.

My father urged me to eat the meal that had been laid upon a mat for us. Palace food: meats I did not recognize, sweet morsels of potato and tomato cooked to perfection, delicate cakes. My eye saw the exquisiteness of its preparation, but fear rendered it tasteless in my mouth. I forced myself to chew, for I knew I would need my strength for the task ahead.

I ended with a vessel of the foaming chocolate that was the drink of the elite; only the very wealthy could afford it. To me it looked as dark as Mictlan and tasted as bitter as death.

Once the core had dried I stuck wax upon it, bulking it up piece by piece until it was entirely covered. This I started to sculpt.

When night came, I felt I had barely begun my task. I would have continued, but the fire of our charcoal burner was not sufficient to light my work. It was as well I stopped for a slave girl – who moved so softly that even my father had not heard her – pulled aside a drape and set more food down for us. When we had eaten, my father and I wrapped ourselves in the warm cloaks provided by our emperor and settled on our mats to rest.

Sleep was slow to come.

From another courtyard floated the beat of a drum and the whistle of pipes. Whoops and yells of laughter greeted the emperor's jugglers and acrobats as they leapt and spun before the nobility. Somewhere in the city my own brother was perhaps being entertained in a similar manner. Thinking of Mitotiqui I curled into a tight ball, trying to ease the pain that twisted in my stomach.

The revelry carried on late into the night. And when that had ceased, the cries of caged coyotes echoed mournfully through the palace, and the low growls of panthers – snarling, furious – seemed to rumble through the ground beneath me like a distant earthquake.

It took me nearly all of the next day to carve the wax to my satisfaction. When I had finished, I stood back and looked at the figure. With a gasp I saw that the face I had crafted to represent the perfect youth was not a likeness of Mitotiqui at all. It was of the youth I had seen in my vision: a face that was not of this world.

Puzzled at what my unconscious mind had made my hands produce, I reached for the face, thinking to refashion it, but my father stayed my hand.

"The work is good, Itacate. And you have no time to change it."

Sighing, I set about covering the whole with clay to make the mould, but my father took my work from me, saying, "This much I can do, Itacate. Sit. Eat. You have a second figure to make. How will you do it?"

It was an apt question. While I ate a chilli-stuffed tamale I started to consider.

Quetzalcoatl was many things: the maker of mankind, the wind, the spirit of new beginnings, the morning star, the warrior of the dawn. He was the deity from whom all art and knowledge flowed. He alone amongst the gods did not demand the blood sacrifice of people.

By the time I had finished eating, the light was already fading; I could do no more that day. Instead I tossed restlessly on my mat, turning images of Quetzalcoatl over in my mind. I had no time for leisurely consideration: by morning I must know what I intended to make.

All night – or so it seemed – I wondered how best to depict the god.

Quetzalcoatl had once taken human form, this much I knew: bearded, with pale skin. In ancient times he had walked the city streets until Tezcatlipoca had outwitted and banished him. More often he was represented in the shape of a feathered serpent. Which did our emperor wish for?

I could only guess at what lay in his heart. But I had made Tezcatlipoca in human form, so perhaps the second figure should match it.

In the year Mitotiqui and I were born, our emperor had built a shrine in the precinct beside the principal temple to honour Quetzalcoatl. Unlike all other temples, this shrine was of round construction, for he was god of winds, which cannot blow freely where there are corners. Perhaps I should adhere to the same principle.

A circular base then, curled with a writhing serpent. From this, a bearded man rising...

The image grew and formed in my head, and when the priests blew their conches to bring forth the new dawn, I began my work.

While I shaped the form of Quetzalcoatl, the clay surrounding that of Tezcatlipoca dried. My father baked it in the fire, melting the wax and letting it run out. It was ready to be cast.

Neither of us had ever created anything this size. With nervous trepidation we melted sufficient gold and poured it into the mould. With anxious glances we ate our meal while we waited for the gold to cool and set. With utter elation we then broke off the clay to reveal the figure: perfect, splendid, immortal.

"I cannot believe even a Mixtec craftsman could produce anything finer," murmured my father.

"For certain, neither can I," I said. "I think it is the very best I shall ever do." My voice shrank to a fearful whisper. "But is it good enough for our emperor?"

My father made no reply.

It was his task to finish it: setting the obsidian in the god's hand and removing the sprues which stuck up from the holes into which we had poured the gold. When all this was done he began rubbing the figure to a bright, lustrous sheen.

122

While my father polished, I laboured to complete the second statue.

In two days more, Quetzalcoatl was likewise finished. It was time to present our work to the emperor.

My father sent a slave to fetch Axcahuah. When the nobleman appeared, he made no comment, but simply summoned slaves to carry the weighty figures. Hidden from view beneath draped cloths, they were borne through the palace towards the emperor, and towards our fate.

As we approached the steps leading to the emperor's chamber, I began to shake. I held the basket of goods I had brought from the market; it seemed a long time ago that we had come here. If all went well, we could return home. If not…

While I had worked, the craft had taken all of my attention. But now I felt dread: my father's life – my life – hung by a thread. If these objects were not approved, then death was certain.

We were preparing to enter the throne room, sinking to our knees, when I heard a voice ringing out in anger. Axcahuah paused, uncertain of what to do. I could hear the words quite clearly. We all could.

"*You* say Quetzalcoatl; yet *he* says Tezcatlipoca.

And now *you* disagree with both of them! *You* tell me that he who leads these strangers is merely a man! Why can you not all agree?"

It was the emperor – no other man could speak with such command. And yet his voice was not the rich, melodious one that we had heard previously. Fury – or fear – made him shrill.

I heard no replies, but someone must have answered, for the emperor spoke again.

"You all chatter until my head rings, but none of you says anything worth hearing! You are advisers. Why do you not advise? Why can none of you tell me what to do? Be gone!"

A commotion followed, and swiftly one, two, three noblemen appeared from behind the screen, their faces flushed and anxious. Axcahuah looked as though he was going to lead us away; it did not seem a propitious moment to approach the emperor.

But then Montezuma called out, "Axcahuah! Where are you? Where is the goldsmith?" and the screen was removed. We had no choice but to edge towards the throne.

When the slaves had set the statues on the floor and retreated from the chamber, my father shuffled towards the first one and pulled away the cloth that covered it.

Axcahuah spoke for him. "My lord," he said, his

voice tight with apprehension, "the work is finished. I hope it finds your favour."

There was silence for a long time, broken only by the sound of the emperor's soft sandals padding like a stalking jaguar around the figure of the god.

Then he asked curtly, "The other? Let me see that of Quetzalcoatl."

On his knees my father approached the second statue and pulled away the covering cloth.

The same silence. The same menacing tread of feet circling.

And then at last the emperor expelled a sigh, though whether of exasperation or contentment I could not tell. My insides shrivelled to a tight knot. Metal cords seemed to bind my chest, making breathing pained and hard.

After a long time he said, "The work is excellent."

Relief rose in me so strongly that I seemed to float to the ceiling.

"Axcahuah, see this man is well rewarded. Give him rich cloths, cloaks, cotton, cocoa beans. Clothes for himself and his family. See he is well supplied with food. He must want for nothing."

We were released.

We entered the temple precinct together, my father's hand clasped unsteadily upon my shoulder. Halfway across he began to shake so violently that he was compelled to sit down; and there, under the full gaze of every passer-by, he wept. I stood in front of him, trying to shield him as best I could.

"I have never been so afraid, Itacate! You are your mother, born again. I could not bear—"

He said no more. Sobs tore his throat, making him incapable of speech. I saw then that my father's reserved detachment in the early years of our childhood had not come from indifference as my brother and I had always supposed. It was not that he cared for us too little, but that he feared for us too much. I stood watching his tears spill, coursing down his cheeks, and felt a pricking at the back of my own eyes. For, had it come sooner, what difference might this knowledge have made to Mitotiqui?

My father calmed himself, and at last we reached a canoe. Heavily laden with tokens of the emperor's favour, we continued our journey home.

As we entered the house, Mayatl clucked over us like an excited chicken. We could tell her nothing, and she had sense enough not to question us. But our unexplained absence had terrified her, and her hands trembled as she laid simple food on mats before us. In my great relief to be home, it tasted more delicious to me than any of the spiced delicacies the palace cooks had conjured up for us.

Creating the figures, I had been kept so busy I had not had time to dwell on the meaning of our lord's tears, or wonder why we had been forced to work in such secrecy. But in the safety of my father's workshop I turned my attention to these questions.

Our life on earth is controlled by two calendars: the temporal and the sacred. The temporal calendar, which governs the turn of seasons and the farmers' year, runs for three hundred and sixty-five days; the sacred, which dictates the round of rites and festivals, for two hundred and sixty. Only once in every fifty-two years do these two calendars conjoin. When they do, it brings to a close the bundle of years. Then – if the gods wish it – a new cycle commences with feasting and celebration; temples are faced with new stone; houses are painted or rebuilt. It is a time of fresh beginnings, of new life, of great optimism.

And if the gods do not wish it? What then?

The bundle of years was currently drawing to an end. In exactly one hundred days the calendars would collide.

I began to suspect that the ill omens of the past years had not been single events, but parts of a larger whole. The night fire in the sky; the burning of temples; the weeping woman; the fireball; the flood... And now the rumours ran that strangers had come to the distant eastern shore.

Our lord emperor was a learned man, as well able to study and interpret the sacred calendar and heavenly portents as any priest. Had he seen the shape of what was to come? Why had he spoken so loudly of Tezcatlipoca? Of Quetzalcoatl? Why – from all the many gods – had he compelled me to fashion these two?

An ancient legend stirred in my mind. Together Tezcatlipoca and Quetzalcoatl had created this world, ripping apart the body of the earth goddess to separate land from sky. Quetzalcoatl had then made mankind to dwell upon it. But he had been tricked by Tezcatlipoca, and the people he had created had then turned upon him and shamed him into leaving. Long ago Quetzalcoatl had vanished into the eastern sea – but not before he had promised to return. And not before he had vowed vengeance on the people of the city who had betrayed him. He would one day come back to Tenochtitlán. With him would come suffering. Without mercy. Without relief.

Without end.

Suddenly weak with fear, I thought I began to see the direction the emperor's mind had taken. This tale was more than an ancient legend; it was a prophecy. Was it soon to be fulfilled? The strangers who had come... Was Quetzalcoatl even now standing on the eastern shore? The figures I had made... Would they be sent as gifts to him?

I put my fingers to my throat to quell my rising panic. It could not be so! The work of my hands sent to a god? It was not possible!

But even as I dismissed my thoughts as insane delusions, new questions burst forth. Would the god know who had made the statues? Could they delay Quetzalcoatl's vengeance? Or would they only serve further to inflame his wrath?

12

The palace was a vast complex, peopled with many nobles and slaves. Though he strove to contain the secrets his messengers carried within those walls, the emperor could not do so, any more than he could force the gods to do his bidding. Rumours began to leak from the court like water from a cracked jar. It was said that the strangers had turned their faces inland and were journeying towards Tenochtitlán. Whispered reports pooled like puddles in the streets; anyone who walked outside could not avoid treading in them.

We did not need to work. My father and I had been so spectacularly paid by the emperor that we had no need to do anything. But without occupation, my thoughts lingered on Mitotiqui. His absence was a constant sorrow, an endless dull pain that penetrated to my core. The house seemed to echo with emptiness now he was gone, and in thinking of what was to become of him I felt I would run mad with woe.

And so I urged my father to let me accompany him to the market, where he might purchase stones. By setting myself a task, I thought I could better bear my distress.

He chose not to buy from Popotl, wishing to keep far from his curious stares, but the trader came in pursuit of us when we approached another merchant.

"Oquitchli!" he said, slapping my father between his shoulders. "I feared for you when you left so hastily. Is all well?"

"Yes," replied my father. "All is well, I thank you." He said no more and turned away, but Popotl was not so easily deterred.

"The nobleman – Axcahuah I think is his name? He had a commission for you?"

My father gave a dismissive shrug. "A trinket, that was all. Some small piece with which to adorn his favourite wife."

"Interesting." Popotl smiled and drew closer. "You have heard the news? You know there is talk of newcomers in this world of ours?"

"Idle gossip," declared my father. "I give it no

credence. From where on the earth could they come?"

"But that is the point! Believe me, Oquitchli, the rumours are true. People are saying that those who come are not of this world. They may be immortals. I have lately been at my home in Cholula. I saw the emperor's messengers with my own eyes journeying east, carrying splendid gifts to them."

"Is that so?"

"Indeed. They sought to evade notice, but it is hard to conceal offerings of such magnitude." Popotl gave a small sigh. "Strange! Two of the pieces looked remarkably like your own. At least, like the work you have done lately. I do not recall your craftsmanship was always so fine." I felt his eyes upon me and burned hot with the fear of what he seemed to know. He gave a loud laugh. "But there! My eyes are not what they were. I must have been mistaken."

My father replied coldly, "You were."

Popotl continued, "The strangers – are you not curious to know from where they come? In Cholula they are already celebrating. They believe it to be Quetzalcoatl himself, for has not legend long foretold he would return? The people of my city believe the god comes to free them from the emperor's mighty fist. No wonder Montezuma seeks to buy their favour. How he must quake to know a god is

132

coming to wrest the throne from him!"

My father said nothing, for what reply could he possibly give? This news was so startling to him that he was rendered speechless.

But hearing it, I felt a sudden, strange relief. My mind was not running mad with deluded imaginings. I had seen clearly what was to come. The ending of the fifth age; the coming of Quetzalcoatl. I could almost hear the calendars as they ground towards the fateful date...

Catastrophe lay ahead and we were powerless to prevent it. All we could do was bow our heads and wait.

In the days that followed, I was too restless to work, either in my father's workshop or in the kitchen. Dread made me clumsy. When I dropped a bowl of freshly ground corn, spilling it across the floor, Mayatl sent me out of the house.

"Go. Bathe. Be massaged. The scented oils may soothe you a little."

Every dwelling in our city, from the humblest peasant's hut to the proudest noble's mansion, had its own bathhouse where its inhabitants could wash daily. In addition, there were the grand public baths – the steam houses – where one could go to be massaged as well as cleansed, with large heated chambers and deep pools of fresh mountain water. Not knowing what else to do with myself, I took Mayatl's advice. But the news I heard at the bathhouse served only to agitate me further.

I had entered the steam room, and was sitting stiff and irritable upon one of the long benches, when in came a portly woman, bristling with the importance of a new rumour.

"Have you heard?" she said, her voice shrill with excitement.

The other women in the chamber were little interested. They looked at her wearily, expecting some trifling tale of a domestic mishap. When she continued she had the great satisfaction of seeing their jaws drop open in amazement.

"There has been a battle!" she announced with relish.

"A battle? Impossible! It is not the season for war!" A woman in the corner dismissed her words in scathing tones.

"Season or not," she persisted, "this force of strangers has fought the Otomi."

"The Otomi?" I echoed, astonished. I knew of their reputation. They were a wild, brutal race whose territory lay next to that of the Tlaxcalans. Their women were as savage as their men, walking abroad with blue-painted breasts bared for all to see.

The Otomi were said to be unconquerable, ungovernable. Certainly our emperor had always allowed them to do as they wished. "These strangers must be fools indeed if they sought a fight with them!"

A woman next to me agreed. "Then it is the last we shall hear of these newcomers. They must have perished."

The portly one shook her head furiously, cheeks flapping like the wattles of a rooster as her words fell over themselves in her hurry to get them out. "No no no – it was the Otomi who perished. The Otomi who were vanquished. It was the strangers who won."

"I heard their numbers were small," puzzled a girl sitting opposite me. "A few hundred. How can they have beaten the Otomi? That tribe has many thousands of warriors."

"They have great magic, it seems. Monstrous dogs that will tear a man's throat out at their bidding. An instrument that will kill ten men with one blow, scattering their limbs to the wind. Sticks that will slay across such a distance that a warrior has no chance even to raise his cudgel against an opponent. How can any fight against such unnatural force?"

The steam chamber seemed suddenly to cool. Every woman sat, arms wrapped around her body, as if seized with cold. There was silence for a while, and then the girl who faced me across the room said quietly, "They are gods, then."

The rooster-cheeked woman was unnerved. She pulled her head back, and then thrust it forward again. "Perhaps," she conceded.

"Quetzalcoatl," said the girl. "It can be no other."

"I know not," came the response. "But it is said their leader has no taste for sacrifice. That has the sound of Quetzalcoatl, does it not? And if they *are* merely mortal, they surely have a powerful god behind them. Some deity smooths their path. How else could they conquer the Otomi? Whatever they are, I think we shall soon find out." She looked about at her fearful audience, timing her next words to cause a sensation. "They have already journeyed far. With each day they come closer. And after their fight with the Otomi, it seems they made an alliance with Tlaxcala. They have their support."

A series of gasps rippled around the chamber. The Tlaxcalans were our ancient foe. Each year the blood of their warriors was spilt on our altars. But now this old enemy had a new and mighty friend...

"What will they do?" I asked softly.

"Who can say? These are peculiar days. But all know the Tlaxcalans have long wanted to rise up against our emperor. If they have the opportunity to do so, they will surely take it."

"They will come here."

"They will," declared the woman. "Only the gods can protect us."

*T*he rumours gripped Tenochtitlán, and when it became certain that the strangers were both real and approaching with an army of Tlaxcalan warriors, people became frozen with fear. No one knew what to say or do. The city quaked with dread at what would follow. We were used to the sights of sacrifice: such suffering was necessary. But if so much blood and pain were required to buy the gods' favour, how much more would be needed now we had lost it?

Our emperor was carried about in his litter as if bidding farewell to the earthly splendours of Tenochtitlán. Before the will of the gods he bowed his head, as did we all, and waited for the blows of fate to fall.

Devastating news came on the next market day.

Mayatl set forth to trade for vegetables but returned almost at once, her face drained of colour, her eyes wide with shock.

"Dead!" she gasped. "Slain!" As she entered the kitchen her knees gave way beneath her and she folded onto the tiled floor.

"Who?" I demanded, panic stripping me of sympathy. Shaking her by the shoulders, I roused her sufficiently to relate the appalling tale.

It seemed there had been a massacre in a nearby city. The strangers had drawn their weapons on the people of Cholula. Unprovoked. Undeserved. Unarmed.

Women. Children. Babies.

Thousands upon thousands of them. Slain without warning. Without mercy.

Knowledge of this slaughter settled on Tenochtitlán like heavy frost. It chilled every heart and filled every belly with despair. My own insides heaved with distress.

And with this dreadful event came even greater confusion. I had thought it certain that he who drew ever nearer was Quetzalcoatl. And yet I knew that the people of Cholula venerated this god above all others; they were his favoured ones, his chosen race. It was inconceivable that he would set upon them and slay them within the precinct of his own temple. The strangers had used their weapons not on warriors but on nobles, merchants, traders, craftsmen. And their Tlaxcalan followers had looted and pillaged the city, burning and destroying until its buildings were ash, its avenues choked with rubble.

With every heartbeat the same questions fluttered inside my head like the wings of a caged bird. It was not Quetzalcoatl ... and yet who but a god could do such things? Who but a god could allow this to happen? Had the Cholulans erred in their beliefs? Had they given their devotion to the wrong deity?

Was this their punishment?

Cholula was ten days' journey from Tenochtitlán. Before the blood had even dried in the streets the strangers and their Tlaxcalan followers marched towards us.

The emperor's spies could be seen scurrying daily to and from the city, and dreadful news swept outwards from the palace like a great wave. The emperor sent more and more gifts, no longer troubling with secrecy or discretion in his growing agitation. It was said that those who approached had a disease – a terrible affliction – that gold alone could cure. The goldsmiths' district of Azcapotzalco was emptied of its ornaments by imperial command as Montezuma sought to buy the strangers' favour.

My father and I did not escape attention. The contents of our own workshop were taken by Axcahuah, who came himself, bursting in so suddenly that I was caught kneeling, moulding a figure in wax. In haste I concealed the object within a fold of my skirt and began to rub the floor with the hem as though attempting to clean it. It was a poor sham, and would not have deceived anyone who looked at me, but Axcahuah did not even glance my way. His mind was filled with more pressing concerns.

"I will take everything now," he told my father. "Payment shall follow later."

In just a few moments all we had – both finished and unfinished pieces, quills of gold, unpolished stones waiting to be set – was loaded into the arms of slaves and taken away to the palace. The workshop was stripped bare; we would have to sit idle until the next market day, when traders would bring more gold.

"These are gifts, my lord?" my father questioned.

Axcahuah frowned at his impertinence, but gave an answer. Perhaps it relieved him to talk of it.

"Our lord emperor offers tribute."

"Tribute?" My father was astonished. Tribute was something paid to our emperor, something given to a conquering force. And yet our warriors had fought no battle. "Do they come to rule us, then?"

Axcahuah shook his head, but his eyes told a different story. "They say they come in peace; our emperor is not so certain. And so he offers them much gold – a price he will pay annually – if they will agree not to enter our city."

"And yet they still come?"

"They do. They say they are envoys of a great ruler. They come to offer our emperor friendship."

"Who is this ruler?" My father's question was little more than a whisper.

In reply the nobleman simply shook his head, and shrugged his shoulders helplessly. He made no further comment, but left our workshop without another word.

The unanswered question lingered in the strange emptiness of the room. My father and I could do nothing but exchange looks, and see our own alarm mirrored in the other's face.

Who claimed to be equal with our emperor? Did such a ruler truly exist? And if he did, how could it be that we had never heard of him?

Like so many of the citizens of Tenochtitlán, my father and I were drawn daily to the great temple precinct to hear the fresh news that flowed from the palace.

One day, soon after dawn, we saw a messenger

leading a procession of many bearers away towards the causeway carrying the finest tokens our city could muster.

The sun was not yet high when I saw that same messenger return. I knew him only by the colour of his cape, for he was in disarray, his eyes rolling in alarm, his hair unbound, clutching at his heart as though it might burst from his chest. He staggered towards the palace, but before he could reach it he fell, almost knocking me off my feet. When I bent to aid him, he grasped my waist as though engulfed in horror.

The bearers who had followed him I now saw were empty-handed and stood confused, uncertain what they should do.

"Can I help you?" I asked gently, trying to prise his arms away from me. A crowd had begun to gather around us to witness this bizarre sight. "Let me assist you into the palace."

"No!" he gasped. "I fear to relate what I have seen to our lord emperor. Is not a teller of bad omens always slain?"

I was too shocked to answer. Before I could reply, he was hoisted to his feet by palace guards and dragged inside. His wailing cries could be heard as he vanished within.

"I have seen the god! The city is doomed!"

The bearers followed, muttering amongst themselves. With these overheard remarks, it did not take long for the tale to be pieced together by the assembled crowd. I had not moved from the precinct before I knew what had occurred.

It seemed the messenger had never reached the strangers. Indeed he had barely crossed the causeway with his gifts, when he had found his path blocked by an aged man with jaguar-clawed toes, apparently sleeping in the road.

The messenger had tried to rouse this withered ancient, but as soon as he had touched him the old man had vanished. Startled, the messenger had looked about him, and the old man had appeared on the road ahead, grinning with mad delight. Whirling his walking stick above his head, he had begun to cackle.

At once the skies had darkened and a wind had blown about them, tearing at their fine cloaks and making the bearers spill their goods upon the ground, where they went rolling into the lake. And then the wizened creature had pointed back along the causeway to Tenochtitlán. As he had watched, the messenger had seen our city burst into flames before both vision and old man disappeared.

This tale swept through the crowded streets. Men wept openly with despair. Women held their

144

children to their breasts in passionate frenzy, kissing them fiercely as though for the last time.

The name of the god was on every tongue. I had to press my hand to my lips to stop a sob bursting from me. Had I not seen him myself in the market-place? Had not Mitotiqui shielded me from his blows? Had I not carved his waxen image?

No one could doubt that the old man who had thus foretold the destruction of our city was Titlacuan, the destroyer: the dark face of the god Tezcatlipoca.

*T*he strangers had gathered on the shore. In the evening light we could make out little detail, but the immense size of the force assembled against us was in no doubt. We were surrounded: held within Tenochtitlán by Tlaxcalans who had massed at the end of each causeway, and who swarmed upon the hills, numerous as ants. And as we watched they stood in turn, each raising his cloak high so that a blood-red wave rippled across the slopes.

With fear gnawing at my insides, my father and I elbowed through the crowds that were drawn to the city's edge to view this spectacle. Each mouth muttered different words, but the meaning was always the same: terror, doom, death.

"The entire Tlaxcalan army is there!"

"Listen! They give their battle cry!"

"Why does our emperor not send warriors to defend us?"

"It is not the season of war."

"The rituals have not been observed."

"The priests will not allow it."

"The gods have decided our destiny. Our lord emperor knows that no warriors can protect us from it."

"We can do nothing."

"We must accept our fate."

They made no move that day.

Darkness fell heavy on Tenochtitlán, and silence gripped the city as though every person within held their breath. For this was the night when the sacred and temporal calendars became aligned. It was the close of the bundle of years. As was the custom, all fires were extinguished to mark its end. At dawn a new cycle would begin.

Or it would not.

I had no thought of sleep. Though I lay on my reed mat, I was so afraid I knew I could not rest. Mayatl had turned her face to the wall but neither did she slumber. Her breathing came hard and fast, labouring under the weight of apprehension. I believed we would remain like this until dawn, but suddenly sleep came upon me, enveloping me so swiftly it was as though I had drunk deep draughts of pulque.

I dreamt of the same youth I had seen when Mitotiqui and I had eaten the sacred mushrooms. His hair came from his head in curves, twisting and writhing like serpents, and yet I knew full well that a man's hair grows straight no matter how he wears it. It was strangely coloured too, not black but gleaming gold, and his eyes were not brown but the blue of the sky, the blue of the lake. This youth said nothing. Merely looked at me. When I woke – suddenly, with a gasp – I was chilled with cold, as though a wind had blown from the mountain tops into my bedchamber. My heart pounded – not with fear but with a sensation so akin to it, it was hard to identify.

I sat up. It was so still that when the dawn flushed the sky with gold, the sounds of clanking metal, dogs barking, men shouting, could be faintly heard from the distant shore.

Scarcely stopping to dress and eat, my father and I left the house, joining the crowds that hastened towards the causeway, where a cataclysm would shortly come to meet us.

They approached. Conquerors of the Otomi; destroyers of Cholula. Led by the god, perhaps, or at least one smiled on by Tezcatlipoca. Behind them, all the warriors of Tlaxcala.

If the moon had stepped from the sky and bathed in the lake, if the sun had climbed down from the heavens and walked into Tenochtitlán, it could not have amazed us so much as what came on that crisp, bright morning.

The whole city, from slave to noble, had been drawn into the streets to see them. The lake was choked with canoes that sat dangerously low in the water, so full were they of terrified onlookers. The rooftops were tightly packed, the streets near impassable. And over all this great throng hung an awful quiet that was punctuated only by the wail of a baby, the cry of a child, a soft low moan from a woman who could not contain her anxiety.

The tramp of many feet broke it. Though they were some way off, we heard their advance long before we could see the faces of those who came. I watched, feeling a cold detachment from the scene, for fear had numbed me. My father and I had walked onto the causeway to better see their progress. As the distant shapes took form, I noted that these strangers had an eye for spectacle – for drama and pageantry – that rivalled our own. Wishing to strike dread and awe into our hearts, they had arranged themselves with artful care.

149

At the head of the procession came four beasts the like of which neither I nor anyone in Tenochtitlán had ever seen. Creatures whose shoulders stood taller than a man. Whose iron feet struck sparks off the stones they clattered over. From whose nostrils plumed smoke as though they breathed fire. And on their backs, men with skin of an oddly pale hue, dressed in polished metal that gleamed in the sunshine. The men of the Aztec empire are smooth-faced, but these newcomers had thick beards upon their chins that were cut into a point at the end like the god Quetzalcoatl. It was easy to see how our messengers had taken them for immortals. They seemed not of this earth. Waving metal knives with blades as sharp as obsidian and longer than a man's arm, they advanced, and people shrank back to make way for them.

As the crowds shifted and rearranged, I found myself pushed to the front. No one stood between the mighty procession and me. If I reached out a hand, I could touch them. My eyes drank in every detail. Each fresh sight pressed upon my mind, leaving an imprint as deep and clear as if my head was filled with soft wax. I found I could not feel fear, although all around me seemed to quake with it. Only a wild excitement held me. I was aware that if they came to fight, I would be amongst the first slain; but I could not bring myself to care. I was stunned by the splendour of those who passed. Curiosity inflamed me.

A man came carrying a length of bright cloth upon a pole which he twirled as he walked, letting the material flow out behind him in display. Then followed others on foot, plumed helmets glinting, weapons held as if ready for battle. Men with bows of a strange crossed construction which would surely fire the arrows that were bunched, bristling, at their hips. They were not like the longbows of our own warriors, but I did not doubt that theirs were the more deadly.

Behind them came three dark-skirted men who had styled their hair in an outlandish way by cutting a neat circle from their crowns. Each carried a painted wooden figure. That in the front was of a dying man fixed to a cross. Behind him a woman, robed in the blue of sacrifice, with a baby in her arms. Last was a well-muscled man who carried a small child upon his shoulder. From the care and reverence with which they held them, I took these to be their gods.

Suddenly several huge dogs – large enough to knock a warrior off his feet – were released from the lines of the procession and ran amongst the gathered crowds. Their teeth were so long they could rip a throat out with one tearing bite. Slobbering, panting, urinating, they caused panic wherever they went. The strangers made no attempt to control their creatures, but rather seemed to relish the alarm that spread in waves before them.

One such beast ran straight at me – a hound whose head came up to my chest. I recoiled, flinching, pressing back, but there was such a mass of people I had nowhere to flee. Without warning, the creature leapt, placing a clawed paw on either shoulder. It was so heavy that my knees threatened to buckle beneath me.

Here was my death. Here. Now.

I waited for those teeth to close upon my throat. With its dreadful breath rank and hot in my face, it opened its cavernous mouth, its lips curled back to expose those savage fangs – but then its tongue came out and I was licked across the face. Revolted, relieved, I pushed the dog away, wiping my mouth with the back of my arm. The men who rode by laughed at my discomfort and I bristled with fury.

More of the huge iron-footed beasts came. Five abreast, and then five more. And between them a man on a white mount whose armour was polished so highly that it blinded the eyes of any who looked at him. From their grouping, and the attitude of reverence shown by those who surrounded him, I guessed this was their leader.

As he drew level with me, he stopped. I could not – would not – drop my gaze. Was he the god? Was he Tezcatlipoca? I stared, longing to know the truth. Slowly the man turned and scanned the bent heads of those that lined the causeway. For a moment, his eyes met mine. And in that instant I knew he was a man. I had seen the god: at the spring festival I had been scalded by the glory of his gaze. This man was not Tezcatlipoca, nor was he possessed by his spirit. For certain his eyes blazed as if fired by some great emotion, but those pupils were as mortal as mine.

Behind him was a column of Tlaxcalan warriors painted for battle, screaming their war cries and giving wild yelps and whistles. There were so many thousands of them that their line extended back all the way to the lake shore.

Those at the head of the procession had already entered Tenochtitlán. Now the ranks of those who were still on the causeway divided. Our emperor was coming forth! He was coming out of the city to welcome these strangers!

The causeway was wide, but it was now so full that our emperor's progress was slow. He came carried on his litter, with few attendants, humbly as it seemed to me, to honour these intruders.

When he stepped out, all around him tried to kneel, but the mass of bodies was so great that none could do so. All cast their eyes to the ground and covered their faces with their hands. I averted my gaze, turning my head once more towards the foreign leader. From where had he come? In what unknown land did he make his home?

In a strange tongue he addressed our emperor. His words were translated by the slave who attended him.

"You are the emperor? You are ruler of this city?" he demanded roughly.

Acknowledging that it was so, our emperor spoke the formal words of courtesy that were always extended to guests.

"My lords, you have travelled far; you are weary." His voice sounded forced, wooden, as if he tried to make his words sincere. Gesturing to the city behind him, he said, "My palace is now your home. Come rest your aching limbs. Come eat your fill. You are my most honoured guests."

To my very great shock, this man in dazzling armour then sprang down from his mount. Before I could look away, he boldly put his arms around our emperor – laid hands upon him – and kissed him on both cheeks! I dropped my head in horror and embarrassment. I alone had seen. But the people around me had heard the noise of the embrace and the slap of foreign lips upon our emperor's face.

As one they took a sharp indrawn breath.

It was then that I first became aware of a dreadful smell. I had come across it only once before, and it was some time before I could recognize it. Long ago, Mitotiqui and I had stumbled across what we took to be a pile of old rags. It had turned out to be a person – a man sick in his mind – who had lain in the streets for several days, unattended and forgotten. This was the smell that now hung all around me: sweat, unclean clothes and unwashed bodies. These strangers stank worse than their animals!

It seemed that their powerful odour had also reached the emperor's nostrils, for he called to the priests who accompanied him. They came forward, liberally pouring sweet-smelling incense upon our guests to drown their ghastly aroma. Their leader lowered his head graciously, as if a very great honour was being bestowed on him.

From where it came, I know not. Perhaps the dread of the last few months at last overcame me; perhaps I simply could not contain myself any longer, but had to find some means of release. The sight of our priests desperately dousing these strangers with incense while they bowed solemnly as if accepting some noble tribute made a great laugh swell in my chest. It rose until it threatened to burst from my throat. I had to suppress it. It could not

155

escape. Not there, not then! Biting my lip I raised a hand to my mouth to stop the smile that grew, broad and uncontrollable, on my face. Casting my eyes about frantically, I searched for a distraction.

And found one.

In the group of strangers pressed together tightly behind their leader was a youth. A soldier. One who stood out amongst his dark-haired fellows. Whose eyes were the blue of the sky, the blue of the lake. Whose hair came from his head in curves, twisting and writhing like serpents, and which gleamed gold when he turned towards me. And smiled. For, though he was from another world, he had seen my laughter and understood its cause.

In an instant all amusement was wiped from me. Tezcatlipoca had shown me this man's visage twice. Why? To what purpose? In confusion I dropped my eyes. He did not. I felt his gaze pressing against my flesh and flushed hot with the knowledge of it. My heart thudded against my ribs.

The emperor had finished with his courtesies. He was about to show the bearded leader to the rooms that were prepared, when the foreigner took our lord emperor by the arm as though he were a small child, and walked with him towards the entrance to our city. I should have been shocked – mortally insulted – by this, but now I hardly noticed it.

As the procession began to move once more, I looked up. The youth's eyes were still fixed on me, gazing with a searing intensity into my own. As the column marched forward, he turned his head to keep me in view. Only when he stumbled, earning a reprimand from the man behind him, did he finally wrest his eyes from mine.

And then he was gone.

My father and I returned home. We said little. What words existed to describe what we felt? Never had my life been split so clearly into time before and time after. In the space of one day, all had changed. It was as though the ground had been yanked like a reed mat from beneath my feet and I was falling. The city I knew was being turned on its head. The lake was being spun into the sky, the clouds pulled down for me to walk upon.

I could not think – could not believe – that the youth who had gazed at me was anything other than mortal flesh and blood. Yet where had he come from? In what unknown land had he lived? Where on the earth could this new race of men have concealed themselves that we neither knew of nor even imagined their existence?

The strangers had entered the city on Quetzal-coatl's day.

Gods have many shapes and many aspects. On this day the usually benign god is at his most fearsome, taking the form of a tempestuous whirlwind that destroys everything in its path. Our priests tell us that this is a time to be dreaded, for on this night robbers, wizards, murderers and rapists are free to do their worst while their victims lie powerless in a trance-like slumber.

No criminals roamed the streets; no violence was done to anyone. Yet people seemed dazed as though they had been dealt a crushing blow to the head. An eerie quiet thickened the air from sundown to sunrise. And I myself sat as though turned to stone. The face of the youth was branded on my mind; I could not avoid it. I did not want to.

The strangers had been welcomed in the style of honoured guests and were now lodged in the palace. Their Tlaxcalan followers – although dressed for war and painted for battle – had been received by our emperor as if they were their loyal retinue. He had not bowed before them, nor treated them as conquerors, and there was some relief in that. No blow had yet been struck. But whether it would fall this night or the next we did not know.

As we ate the meal Mayatl placed before us, my

father began to murmur, "He let them in. With not one word of protest he let them in! Did you see him, Itacate?"

"I did."

"He let them in and went with them like a child!"

His distress was profound. I had never seen him so unsettled. Never heard him question the wisdom of our ruler.

"He has made a gift of us all. Placed our fate in the hands of strangers. He may as well have given us all to be slaves."

"It cannot be so. Perhaps they are good men," I ventured. "If they are indeed ambassadors from some distant land—"

"From what land? Where? Our priests have told us the limits of our world! Have they judged wrong? How can that be?"

I could make no answer. Instead I said, "The emperor has spies, has he not? He surely knows more of these strangers than we do. He must feel they are to be trusted."

But my father would not be soothed. "He knows what they did in Cholula. As do you. They have a wild – an unnatural – streak of cruelty threaded through their hearts. He has unleashed a monster in our city! And taken the Tlaxcalans – our enemy – to be his guests."

"Yet they have not struck."

"They do not need to! If they hold our lord, they hold us too. We are helpless now; our emperor has made us so. We must keep far away from them. You too, Itacate. I saw the stare you were given. Do not venture near the palace. You are not to go there. Not on any account. Do you hear me?"

I nodded, for I could do nothing else.

But as I lay on my mat through that long, sleepless night I could neither sweep the image of the youth from my mind, nor wipe the feel of his gaze from my skin.

In the days and weeks that followed, the city's inhabitants moved as though stupefied. With each breath we expected the hand of fate to bring our doom. Yet nothing happened. Life seemed to go on as before. There were changes in the marketplace but I thought at first these were small things, of no great import to anyone but myself.

There was no gold to be had in Tlaltelolco, and those who traded it were absent from the market. It seemed they had been told to take their wares straight to the palace. Our emperor wished to ease the terrible sickness that had brought the strangers to our city in search of a cure.

I felt the loss of gold like an aching tooth. With

none to craft, what purpose did I have? What could distract me from my thoughts? What could ease the gaping wound of my brother's loss? I walked behind my father as he meandered between the sellers of gems and polished stones, but I could see the goods they displayed were of poor quality. I presumed that those of greater value had been poured into the laps of the strangers.

Popotl was not at market. I did not miss him – I disliked the trader – and yet his empty stall unnerved me. Whether he had perished at Cholula, or whether he had delivered his wares in person to the palace, none could say; but whatever the reason, it was the strangers who had caused his absence.

As I cast my eyes about me, I saw more that coloured my mind with disquiet. Those who traded fruit and vegetables had laid their produce on reed mats as they always did. But it seemed to me that the tomatoes were piled less high, the sweet potatoes spread more thinly, the chillies less abundant than they had ever been. The strangers numbered a few hundred men, their Tlaxcalan followers many thousands. They were all our guests. With so many extra mouths to feed, much produce must have been delivered to the court. For now – so soon after the harvest, when the grain stores were full – our supplies would be sufficient. But how long were these foreigners to reside in our city? When winter began to bite, how would we feed them? How many would go hungry to provide hospitality to those we had never invited?

Troubled, we at last came to the edge of the market. My father was empty-handed. Sighing, he said, "We should go home. There is nothing here for us today."

Only then did I remember that I had promised Mayatl I would bring meat for our noonday meal. "I must go back!" I replied. "I told Mayatl—"

I did not finish my sentence. Over my shoulder my father had seen something that caused him such alarm that he seized me by the arm and pushed me ahead of him. Turning, I caught a glimpse of flashing metal. The strangers had come to market and were striding amongst the stalls, examining the wares.

"Our meal!" I gasped as my father propelled me before him, away from the square. "Mayatl wished me to return with meat."

"I have no fancy for meat today," he snapped. "Let us have fish instead. You trade for it in this direction, do you not?"

He steered me along the street that led to the lake shore. But when we came to the place where the fishermen moored their canoes, a disturbing sight met our eyes.

The tall willow trees that had once given such pleasant shade had been felled. They lay stripped and bare, split into long, thin planks. And those who had cut them down and now worked them into the shape of large canoes were not men of Tenochtitlán, but strangers.

O ur meal was a meagre, quiet one, and so we heard the approach of Axcahuah long before he set foot in our house. The tinkling of his bells announced his arrival, but still he called loudly as he crossed the threshold, demanding my father's attention.

"Goldsmith!"

My father stood. "I am here, my lord. You are welcome. Will you eat with us?"

Axcahuah brushed aside my father's courtesies as if batting away noisome flies. With no preceding civilities he stated, "You are ordered by the emperor to come to the palace."

Fear spasmed across my father's face. "Now, my lord?"

"No. On the morrow. You have time to gather

such tools as you will need. Our emperor wishes you to make another figure."

"Another?" My father was astonished. "Were not two sufficient for his needs?"

Axcahuah snapped angrily, "Do you question the will of Montezuma? Are you reluctant to do his bidding?"

"No, my lord!" my father replied hastily, bowing his head. "I know well the great honour he gives this humble goldsmith. With all reverence I shall do as I am commanded."

Somewhat soothed, the nobleman spoke again. "He wishes to present a gift to our guests. It seems they have their own gods. Montezuma commands that a figure be made to honour the deity who steered them to our city."

My father nodded. "It shall be done, my lord. I will come. My daughter will accompany me to fetch and carry, for she can do so with discretion."

I marvelled at the skill with which my father slid me into the scheme; but it was not to be.

"No," the noble replied curtly. "This commission is no secret. There are slaves to run such errands as you wish. The girl stays at home."

Axcahuah left as swiftly as he had come and my father went to his workshop. His pale face and grey lips spoke eloquently of his terror at what was to come, yet he gave me not one look or word of reproach. But I berated myself. Accused myself. Hated myself. I raged at malicious Tezcatlipoca, who had given me the talent that should have belonged to Mitotiqui. My misplaced skill had condemned not only my brother but also my father.

Quietly he gathered what tools he would need and laid them out on the floor. Slowly, with trembling hands, he rolled them in a cloth for the morning. Then he said, "I will go into the city, Itacate. I feel the need to walk."

"Do you wish for company?"

"No. I will go alone."

He left me, shoulders hunched, back bent, looking suddenly old and frail. He did not return until after sunset, going straight to his chamber without a word.

That night I lay in the dark, dreading what would happen. It tore at my throat with teeth as sharp as those of the mighty dogs who did the strangers' bidding. Unable to sleep, at last I crossed the courtyard. Kneeling before the household shrine, I pricked my flesh with thorns until the hot blood flowed. Reverently, desperately, I begged the gods to show me some way to evade the coming disaster.

When the night was at its blackest, the chill

breath of Tezcatlipoca cooled the heated ardour of my prayers. His cold touch stilled me. And while I sat, motionless, waiting, the god slipped a thought into my head; I saw a plan as clearly as if he had whispered the words in my ear.

My hands had placed my father in danger of his life. My hands alone could save him.

He could not make the statue; I could. But I was a girl. A girl could do nothing, be nothing, go nowhere. Were I a boy I could have gone in my father's place. Had I been born one... Or had I the appearance of one...

The young men of my city wear their hair loose about their shoulders. Only when they have taken captives in battle can they put it up into the warriors' prized topknot. Girls of marriageable age such as myself bind their hair, coiling it tightly at the nape of the neck. If it were unbound, nothing would distinguish mine from my brother's.

A woman's garb is simple: a long shirt and a skirt that reaches to the ground. That of a man is simpler still: a length of cloth about the hips bound in a knot at the groin; and a cloak, tied at the neck, which hangs open at the chest. Yet some prefer to wear their cloaks beneath one arm, and make the knot upon the opposite shoulder. With a large cloak might I not do the same? The generous quantity of cloth would hang in folds, concealing my small breasts. And to ensure the fabric did not fall apart, I could stitch one side to the other.

The risk was great. If I was discovered, I would be killed. Yet my father's death was already certain. His failing sight, his lesser skill, guaranteed it. And when he offended the emperor, was not my own doom equally assured? The words of Montezuma echoed in my ears: *If you once displease me, all trace of you and your family shall be removed from the earth.*

I could not sit meekly and await this fate.

Before the sun rose I dressed myself in the manner of a youth. At first light I slipped through my sleeping father's chamber and crossed the courtyard to his workshop. Taking his tools I went silently from the house. And, not knowing if I had yielded to the god's will or fallen into a malevolent trap of his devising, I set forth for the palace.

*T*he palace had changed since the arrival of the strangers.

Every building in Tenochtitlán is open to the street. From the humblest peasant's hut to the emperor's vast dwelling, there are no barriers preventing entry. Until these foreigners came to our city we had no notion of what a door was. As I stood before the palace, I saw huge planks of wood fastened together to bar the entrance. None might pass through without permission. And those that granted access were not the servants of the emperor, but iron-clad strangers astride their mounts.

Overcome with fear, I knew not how to approach. I might perhaps have turned and fled, but one called to me in my own tongue, and I was compelled to answer.

"You, boy! What do you want here?"

"I come to do the emperor's bidding. The lord Axcahuah sent for me. I am the goldsmith." My throat was so tight with terror that my voice came out high. Girlish. I swallowed several times, trying to moisten the cords of my throat that I might deepen it when I spoke again.

But the strangers paid little heed to my voice. The cry was hurled from man to man until it reached deep into the palace. "Bring Axcahuah! Bid him come to the gates."

I stood astounded at the power of these guests to command their hosts. Then the doors swung open, and the nobleman stepped out to greet me.

He had never once looked at me: of that I was certain. Girls are invisible. He had no notion of who I truly was. Yet what courage it took to look him full in the face! From earliest childhood I had been told to avert my eyes, to lower them, to bow my head. I had done it for so long it had become instinctive. To now raise my chin and meet his gaze without flinching took all the resolve I had.

"You are not the goldsmith," he said brusquely.

"I am his apprentice, my lord. My master has been taken with a sudden sickness. He sent me in his place."

The noble made no answer, but his face twisted with anger.

"I know my master's methods, my lord," I continued urgently. I was sure my father would come in pursuit when he observed my absence. If the god's plan was to succeed I had to enter the palace at once. "He has trained me well. I believe I can work to the emperor's satisfaction."

"I hope you are right," answered Axcahuah, his lips thinned to a tight line. "We shall both pay the price if you fail. As will your master."

Gesturing for me to follow him, he led the way inside. I thought I heard my father's shout, distant across the temple precinct, but I did not turn. The doors swung shut behind us. I was closed in with whatever fate the god planned for me.

The palace interior had also changed. The air that had once been so richly fragrant with sweet blossom had become thick with the aroma of human sweat. Incense had been sprinkled liberally but it was not enough to mask the odour of unwashed bodies. The dogs had been allowed to roam freely, urinating on pillars, defecating in corners; and, though the emperor had many slaves, no amount of cleaning could wipe away the animals' stink. It was worse still in the first courtyard we passed through. Here the gigantic creatures they rode astride were now housed. Their iron-clad hooves had cracked the delicate tiles they stood upon, and the place was awash with urine and dung. The stench was overpowering.

"What are these creatures?" I asked.

"They call them horses." Axcahuah could not disguise his fear of these beasts. He edged carefully past, his shoulder pressed against the wall to keep as far away as possible. When the animal closest to him threw up its head and snorted hot breath in his face, Axcahuah broke into a run. His panic provoked great mirth amongst the strangers and their laughter rang in my ears as I pursued him.

Having left the courtyard, we walked deeper into the interior. The transformation was astonishing. Where once there had been gracious tranquillity and peaceful repose, there was now only the grating noise and raucous laughter of Tlaxcalan men. The jugglers who had daily practised their skills for the nightly entertainment of our emperor now performed in bright, glaring sunshine for the strangers who sat in idle groups to watch them. Sweaty palms were clumsy; as we passed, one dropped a club and was jeered at by his audience.

Then I saw a sight that made me stop. Standing beside these men were women of our city. I watched as a girl no older than I was clasped by one of the foreigners. He pulled her to him and – in full view of all – fondled her breasts. I was aghast, yet her face was a frozen, unfeeling mask as if she had become dulled to such usage. To touch a slave thus would have been shaming enough. But this girl was well dressed; I could tell in a glance that she was high-born, one of the elite. Seeing the direction of my stare, Axcahuah likewise paused.

"Who is she?" I asked.

"Tecpan, niece to Montezuma," he answered coolly. "She is given to them."

"Our emperor gives his niece as a gift?" I asked, horrified.

Axcahuah nodded. "His daughters too. To their leader." He gave a small, throaty grunt that could have been contempt. "Our lord will give anything to buy their favour."

He said no more. It was treason to do so. We could neither of us doubt the judgement of our emperor. But as we continued my heart quaked with misgivings. I felt exposed, sick to the very core of my being with the thought of what these men might do to me if I were discovered. My decision was foolish beyond belief! I had made a grave error in coming here.

Trembling with fear, I followed the noble to the slaves' quarters. He led me to the selfsame place where I had worked beside my father. But no screens now marked off the area where I was to labour. Instead the workspace was bordered by gold: ornaments, jewellery, shields and breastplates all heaped high. There were ancient Mixtec pieces of such exquisite craftsmanship that they stole the breath from me. I was walled in with treasure.

As I stood astonished at the wealth so casually stacked about me, there was a deafening bark. The slobbering hound by whom I had been so disgustingly licked on the causeway leapt at me and I recoiled, nearly falling into a pile of gold. But a sharp word of command recalled the beast and it sat, tail thrashing across the tiles, grinning up at me with its savage teeth. When I looked to see who had saved me, my stomach lurched.

Staring at me from across the courtyard was the youth with curling hair.

Although the youth had gazed with fascination at the girl on the causeway, to the boy before him he barely gave a glance. Indifference was written on his face. A brief nod of greeting was all I received before he turned his attention back to the dog at his side.

It was from Axcahuah that I learnt the reason for his presence.

"As your master has informed you, our lord emperor commands a statue to be made in honour of our guests' gods. This man has been sent by their leader to oversee your work. He will tell you what the figure is to represent."

"How, my lord?" I asked. "Who is to interpret?"

"He speaks our tongue," Axcahuah replied. "I will go now. If there is anything you require, send a slave to me with word."

"I will, my lord." I bowed my head respectfully, and watched as he withdrew. I was left alone with the stranger.

For several pounding heartbeats I stood with my back to him, looking in the direction the nobleman had gone. I lacked the courage to turn and face him. My tongue seemed fixed to the roof of my mouth; my palms sweated; my skin was suffused with sudden heat; my blood rushed not with fear but with an emotion that alarmed me much more. Only when he spoke, smoothly and in my own language, did I recall my purpose.

"Come, let us begin," he said. "We have a task to achieve, have we not? My leader, Cortés, is anxious to see the piece. He is not famed for his patience."

"No more is mine." I swung round. Crushing my resolve into a ball that sat hard beneath my ribs, I said, "You must tell me what I am to make. Which of your gods is to be honoured?"

He did not answer me at once, but took the wooden idols I had seen carried aloft across the causeway from a large chest and set them down before me. Putting my mind firmly to the task, ignoring his close proximity as well as I could, I knelt to examine them.

"We worship the one true god," he said. "The creator of all."

"Only one god?" I echoed, eyebrows raised as I surveyed the figures. At random I picked up the carving of the man who carried a small child upon his shoulder. "Is this your creator god?"

"No ... that is a saint. A holy man. St Christopher is his name. He protects travellers such as ourselves."

"But he is not a god?"

"No."

I pulled towards me another figure – that of the man fixed to a cross. His beautiful face was contorted with pain, his hands and feet pierced with knives that pinned him to the wood. In his side was a wound from which gushed blood.

"That is Jesus," the youth informed me. "He is the son of god."

I looked at the loveliness of that anguished face. He was like Tezcatlipoca. "He is divine... And yet he takes the form of a man?"

"He is a man – was a man. He lived here on earth. But he is also divine. Now he is in paradise."

"But why does he suffer like this? Was he given in sacrifice?"

"He was killed. For our sins. And thus was born our faith."

"In the blood of sacrifice," I muttered to myself.

178

"As was ours. Perhaps our gods are different in name alone." I frowned, struggling to understand. "If Jesus is divine, you must have two gods: father and son. They cannot be one."

"They *are* one. There is a trinity, three in one: father, son, holy spirit." He held his hands up in apology and sighed. "I am sorry. I have not yet sufficient words of your tongue to explain these holy mysteries!"

"No matter. Tell me which of these figures I am to make, and I shall begin."

He leant towards me and pulled the form of the dying man from my hands, replacing it with that of the woman draped in blue. In her arms she held an infant boy.

"This is the madonna," he explained. "The virgin Mary, the mother of god. It is to her our leader most often prays. It is by her grace that we are here. By her favour our two worlds have met."

I was puzzled. This woman was surely the goddess from whose body the earth had been moulded. Here our faiths did not diverge. But why then had he said the creator god was male? "*She* is the creator?" I asked. "The origin of all?"

"No."

I frowned. "Then the baby? He is the one true god you speak of?"

"He is Jesus."

"Jesus? Who was sacrificed? She is his mother?"
He nodded.

"Then why do you call her the mother of god?
Is she not rather his lover?"

The youth threw his head back and laughed. "You
tie me in knots! I cannot explain. I am no priest."

I could not share his laughter; he made me feel
stupid and awkward. Embarrassed, I said quietly,
"If this woman is the one whom my emperor wishes
to honour, I will do his bidding. I shall copy this in
gold."

Rising from the ground, I began to gather the
materials I needed. But he had not finished.

"You find my faith strange," he said. "To me
yours is equally puzzling. Such an array of gods!
And all so fearsome!"

I was stung by his mockery. "Our gods are good
to us," I replied. "They bring us rain. They make the
maize grow."

"And for that they demand the blood of your
people!"

My temper stirred. "Without it the sun cannot
rise!"

He said nothing, but the arch of his eyebrows
incensed me.

"It is necessary!" I told him. "Do you think we

would do these things if it were not? Do you think sacrifice is easy?"

He gave a caustic laugh. "I am sure it is hard to watch," he said. "Yet it is harder still for those that must be put to the knife."

Sudden fury made me reckless. "To die in this way is a great honour! There is constant rivalry amongst the young men. They compete for such a privilege…"

He looked at me assessingly. "Is it an honour you have sought?"

"No! Of course not!" I spat. "How could I — ?" In my rage I had almost told him I was a girl! Swiftly I covered my error with more ill-chosen words. "The young men go willingly, joyfully."

The youth snorted in disbelief.

"It is true!" I shouted. "My own brother is to be honoured in this way. We delight in it! At the spring festival he will — "

I could not continue. Emotion choked my throat; grief contorted my face. I could not disguise it. The youth stared, his eyes piercing mine for long, slow heartbeats until he had read the truth in them and my soul lay bare before him.

"Your brother does not go willingly," he said quietly.

"I did not say that."

"You did not need to."

My eyes blurred with tears. He turned away from me, giving his attention to the dog, and for that I was grateful.

I feared to draw the notice of the god by speaking further. Struggling to compose myself, I reasoned that this alone was why my fingers trembled and my blood rushed so noisily in my ears. It had no connection whatsoever to this youth – this heathen! – who had seen so clearly what I had long kept hidden in my heart.

I had felt the gods' presence when
I had made the figures for our emperor. They had
directed my fingers and filled my soul with the
knowledge and skill to create that which did them
due honour.

It was not so now. I had been abandoned.

I mixed charcoal with clay, and under the
watchful eye of the youth started to craft the statue's core. The pressure of his stare made my fingers
clumsy and talentless. As the long day wore on, my
shoulders ached under the burden; my neck became
stiff with tension; a throbbing pain drummed at my
temples.

At noon a slave girl brought us food. I carried
mine to the far corner of the courtyard and ate alone.
I did not glance at him. Not once. I feared that if I

took just one look at those lake-blue eyes I would be unable to pull my gaze away. And so I studied the tiles. The carved pillars. The Mixtec gold. The strangers' statues of their gods. My eyes roamed anywhere, everywhere, but never towards him. And yet I knew everything that he did; awareness of his movements seeped through my skin. I felt him sample each dish, and pick out morsels for the dog that sat beside him. Knew he smiled when he tasted the foaming chocolate. And when he stretched out in the shade and began to doze, my whole body seemed weakened by an intense, unfamiliar longing.

Only when his breath deepened and slowed did I turn to look at him. Hungrily I consumed every detail: how his hair glinted gold where the sun caught it; how the dark lashes curved against his cheek; how he alone amongst his countrymen kept his pale skin scrubbed clean.

He stirred. Swiftly, I snatched my gaze away and forced my attention back to my task.

At last I finished the core, but not to my satisfaction. Glancing from it to the wooden figurine, I saw I had misjudged the proportions. If I continued and set wax upon it, my finished statue would be a distortion of the original. The goddess would have elongated limbs, a bloated face. And as for the baby in her arms

– it looked more like a demon than an infant!

In anger I pushed it to the ground, crushing the clay beneath my palms until it was flattened. A day's work was ruined in an instant.

The youth spoke. "You were not content?" he asked.

"I was not." Rubbing my temples, I glared at the wooden woman. I had never before struggled with my art. To lose my skill now, at such a time! Tears threatened to spill from my eyes. "I have no understanding of this goddess!" I exclaimed. "My heart does not tell my fingers what to do."

"Will you let me help you?"

"*You?*"

"I was a goldsmith in my own land."

Astonishment made my mouth gape. He smiled at my expression. "Do not be surprised. The men of my race have their trades too."

"Then why have I been called here? Can you not craft such a figure?"

"No. Not alone. I was an apprentice only." He sighed. "Truly I thought my master was a craftsman until I came to this land. The work I have seen here makes my hands feel heavy as a baker's kneading dough. I have no knowledge of your methods. And yet I can help you, if you will permit me. I understand how the virgin should look." He glanced at the mess of charcoal and clay that lay on the tiles.

"Not like that," I said.

"No. You are right to try again. But the light is fading. At dawn you can begin once more. And – with your consent – I will assist you."

I made no protest. The emperor's wrath hung on the horizon like a gathering storm. I did not wish to bring it closer. If I had to work alongside this youth, I would do so. But I would not talk to him. I could not. He was my enemy! How many of my race had he slaughtered at Cholula? I had to quell the turmoil within.

I had been provided with a warm cloak for bedding. Wrapping myself in it, I sat upright, jaw clenched shut, upon a mat. I had thought he would return to the other men now the work was done for the day, but he did not. Instead he lay, head resting on the broad flank of his dog, and began to speak.

"Are you not curious to know where I come from?" he asked.

"No," I lied.

"Will you have no conversation with me?"

"The emperor does not commission me to talk."

He laughed. "Very well," he said. "I see you are determined. You need not reply. Cover your ears if you must, but I wish to speak. I am called Francisco. Do you have a name?"

My treacherous heart seized gladly upon this knowledge, but I gave no answer.

"I shall call you the silent goldsmith, then. I come from across the sea."

I could not help exclaiming. "But how is that possible? At the horizon the sea falls into nothing."

"It does not! There are other lands beyond the horizon. More than you can dream of. I come from a land we call Spain; it is another country. Hot, like this. With many towns and cities."

I was snared, like a bird in a net. My curiosity could not be contained. "Like Tenochtitlán?" I asked.

"No!" he replied. "Dear god, no. I can truly say that there is no city in the world so large or so beautiful as Tenochtitlán. It humbles even Venice."

"Venice?"

"A city famed for its beauty. Built on water, like this one. But nothing like so big, or so beautiful. Or so clean!"

"And your country ... it has an emperor?"

"Yes. He is Charles, the fifth emperor of Spain. A mighty ruler who governs many people and many lands."

I was perplexed. "How can it be that we had never heard of him?"

Francisco turned onto his side, propping his

head on a hand as he answered, "No more had we Spaniards heard of you. We first found this land just a few years ago. We thought it to be a group of islands. It was not until later that we realized it was a great continent. We too are mightily surprised by what we find. You are as new to me as I to you."

There was a pause while we studied each other. He looked at me with the frank openness of one boy talking to another. Yet I could not hold his gaze. I felt uncomfortably hot, yet in the next instant was so cold that my skin prickled with bumps.

To mask my sudden shivering, I asked, "How do you know my language?"

"The journey here took many long months. I listened well. I was considered a fair scholar in my own country; it was not so hard to learn."

I could not resist the temptation to puncture the pride in his voice. "And yet your knowledge has many gaps, for you have learnt from men and warriors."

"What gaps?"

"You know what to call the food that is set before you when you eat, but do you know the words for the corn it is ground from? The stone used to crush it?"

"But these are women's matters, are they not? From whom would I learn them?"

I changed the conversation's direction at once. "Why do you come here? Is it true that you are sick? That you have a disease of the heart for which you seek a remedy?"

Francisco laughed, but the sound was harsh and contained no trace of mirth. "The tale has travelled before us," he replied, and his voice was suddenly sharp. "Yes... You could well say we are sick men."

In the gathering darkness I watched for his reaction to my next words. "They say that gold gives you the cure. Can it really be so?"

Francisco rolled onto his back, a hand pressed to his chest as if to ease a pain there, and looked up at the stars. "If greed is a sickness, then yes, we are all afflicted by it. We are rotten to the core; riddled with disease. Our leader more than any. But believe me, my silent goldsmith, gold does not cure it. It is like drinking salt water: no man is satiated by it. The more he has, the more he needs; the more his mind runs mad with desire for it." His voice then dropped so low, I strained to catch his words.

"It will be the death of us."

20

Our work began at first light. I had lost an entire day's labour, and we were both aware of the urgency of the task. Mixing fresh clay and charcoal, I started to shape the new core.

Francisco said little. His mood had darkened overnight and he had no desire for idle chatter. When we spoke it was of the statue and nothing else. He did not touch it, but made many comments: "The head is too large; you must remove some for the chin" or "Her arm must curve more." Each remark helped me see more clearly the shape of the figure I was striving for. By the time the slave girl brought our noonday meal the core was completed.

There was nothing more to be done until the clay had hardened sufficiently to take the wax. Working beside Francisco, as I had done all morning, had roused my desire to know more of his country. Of him. Try as I might, I could not douse it. This time it was I who began to talk.

Looking at the huge dog at his side, I recalled the tales of the creatures who ripped out warriors' throats in battle. Was this animal truly one of them? Would it soon be set upon the men of my own city?

"Your beast," I said. "Has it killed many men?"

Francisco laughed loudly. "No!" He fondled the dog's ears with affection. "She is a hunting dog, not one of war. And she is a coward, though she looks so fearsome."

"She is yours?"

"She has become mine. I found her in the forest when we first came to this land. We were sent ashore for fresh water. The expedition that was there the year before had left her behind." He chuckled. "She scared me half to death! The sailors had been telling fearful tales of dog warriors who live in the jungle. When she leapt at me out of the bushes I thought my end had come! I fled back to the ship screaming like a simpleton."

"The ship? What is that?"

"A vessel. Like your canoes but much larger. With sails – great cloaks – that catch the wind and drive it across the ocean."

"Like a temple on the water?"

191

"A what? Oh – a pyramid. Yes, I suppose so."

"I see."

"I was running across the beach towards the ship when she caught up with me, knocked me to the ground and licked me. I thought the sailors would soil themselves with laughing. She was so glad to be found! She has been my companion ever since."

"Does she have a name?"

"Indeed. The sailors named her Eve in mockery of me. I made the mistake of once saying the jungle looked like Eden—"

"Eden?"

"The garden of Eden. The world, when it was created, was called Eden. It was peopled with the first man and woman. He was called Adam, and she was Eve. It was a paradise on earth."

"Was?" I asked. "Is it here no longer?"

A cloud seemed to pass across Francisco's face. His mouth was pinched as though he had tasted something foul. "No... It was spoilt." He stood abruptly. "The core is hardened," he said. "We must work once more."

Without speaking, he assisted me with the task of sticking lumps of wax onto the solid core. When it was covered, I picked up my father's tools and began to sculpt.

I could not summon the same confidence with

which I had shaped the figures of my own gods. I was nervous, hesitant, unsure of my subject. Each mark I made needed Francisco's nod of approval before I dared move on to the next. It was slow work. I had achieved little when the light started to fail.

"You struggle to make sense of this piece," he observed.

"I do."

"If you do not succeed..." Francisco said slowly. "Tell me ... in your city what is the price of failure?"

I shuddered, but did not answer him. And yet he seemed to know what threat hung over me.

"We must find a way to give you understanding," he said. "Perhaps you need to comprehend more about what you are striving to create. The madonna is all tenderness. She is the very essence of motherhood." He handed me a spiced tamale, his fingertips brushing lightly against my palm, a careless touch that set my flesh tingling.

"Does your mother live?" he asked.

"No."

"A pity," he said softly. "But do you have no recollection of the love with which she tended you?"

"None."

My brief answers did not alter his line of reasoning. He was not so easily deflected. Leaning against a pillar, he stared up at the fast-appearing stars.

"Every child longs for their mother's care, whether they have it or not. Let that lead you. Your eyes have sought to make a copy; perhaps your feelings will prove a truer guide to your fingers." He turned his gaze from the stars to my face and said quietly, "The heart is a fragile organ, is it not? It must cleave to something."

"Does yours?"

"Yes. Mine was given the day we entered this city. I lost it on the causeway." He paused for a moment, and then said, sighing, "I am a man, the same as you. Do not all men crave a woman's love?"

He looked at me searchingly and waited for me to speak.

But though I opened my mouth, I could find no words. I turned away. In my agony of confusion I could neither meet his gaze nor give him an answer.

21

I dreamt I was held, not in a mother's soft embrace, but in the fierce, hard arms of a lover. My fingers were twined in golden hair, and above me a canopy of green was cast across the blue sky. Slivers of sunlight pierced it, catching the bright feathers of the birds that flew from tree to tree, dazzling as precious stones.

Throwing back my head, I felt the press of lips against my throat. The brush of fingers on my bare skin.

I woke suddenly, and all was dark. The hour was so late that everything in the palace was still. All slept. All but me. I lay wet with sweat, hot with shame at my dream.

I could not – should not – love this youth. He was a barbarian! A savage! Everything forbade it.

195

Custom. Culture. Faith.

Everything.

Everything but my own heart. It beat in a frenzy of desire. It ached with a pain that was as sharp as a new-made wound, as bitter as chocolate, as dizzying as a bite of the sacred mushroom.

Before Francisco had entered the city, Tezcatlipoca had shown me his face. For what reason? As a warning, a temptation, a cruel jest? Was it the god who had so inflamed my passion? Who had filled my head with a yearning so strong that all thought and reason were extinguished? Was this youth to be the bringer of some malign fate?

I could not know what lay in the god's mind. But I was determined to build a barricade around my heart; I would talk no more to Francisco. Rising from my mat, I walked through the empty palace corridors until I came to a fountain which ran with cool, sweet spring water from the mountains. Here I washed the dream kisses from my neck and face. Rubbed away the touch of his hands from my flesh.

I sat beside that soothing trickle until the first conch blasts called the dawn into being. I tried to force all images of Francisco's Eden from my head. Recalling the long-ago dream of my mother, I sought instead to fill my mind with her image. I prayed that her spirit would guide me on the day to come. But as I rose to return to the courtyard where Francisco lay, my hands hung at my sides, uninspired and heavy as lead.

Desperation and lack of sleep rendered me light-headed, and in this state I began my work, my lips forming a desperate prayer that was at last answered. I felt removed from the object before me; it was as though I looked at it from a great distance – as if my labouring hands were not my own. I seemed no more than a vessel, a conduit, for the great creating force that steers all human artistry. With no conscious thought in my head the wax carved fluidly, and with graceful ease the woman began to emerge. Her arms curved tenderly around the infant held in her protective embrace. Her baby son smiled up at his mother, his tiny fingers clasping her dress. Her robes were draped and folded about her with lifelike softness.

I had finished all but the woman's face when the spell was broken by the arrival of Axcahuah.

"I am come to see how your task proceeds," he said brusquely.

"As you can see, my lord, it is near ready to be cast."

He examined my statue with little enthusiasm, saying only, "You are slower than your master. I had thought you would be finished by now. The emperor grows impatient."

I had neither looked at nor spoken to Francisco that day – I had armoured myself against him and did not intend to weaken. But before I could answer the nobleman, Francisco stepped forward.

"The figure is of great complexity," he said calmly. "If we are truly to honour the virgin, her statue cannot be hurried. Cortés will not thank your emperor if he is given an imperfect piece."

Axcahuah was taken aback to be addressed in this way. He frowned, and his lips tightened, but he said nothing. These strangers were the emperor's guests; he was constrained by the rules of hospitality. With some effort, he lowered his head in a slight bow. "I leave you to your work," he said. But his eyes glared into mine as he withdrew, and in them I read a dark warning that filled me with dread.

A slave girl brought food, but I could not eat. I sat down again to carve, but my trance-like state had vanished. My hands felt stiff and clumsy, and when I raised my tools to shape the blank wax they began to tremble. I stared in alarm at the statue's face, smooth and featureless as an egg. I could not sculpt it!

When last I had worked in the palace, I had meant to create the visage of my brother, and failed. If I attempted to proceed now, I knew with sudden certainty that what would emerge from the wax would not be a woman's features, but those of Francisco. I could almost hear the spiteful laugh of Tezcatlipoca. The knife I held dropped from my hands, the stone blade shattering upon the tiles.

Seeing my distress, Francisco set down his food and crossed the courtyard. Kneeling beside me – so close that I felt his breath on my cheek – he examined the statue.

"Such skill! And so little left to be done," he murmured. "Yet the most important aspect is unfinished."

I clasped my hands in my lap in an effort to cease their shaking. It did not escape his attention.

"You are wearied, I think, and now fear has unsettled you." There was a long pause and I felt his eyes sliding over my skin, but kept my own gaze fixed ahead. He said, "I have a favour to ask of you."

I glanced at him, but looked away almost at once. I could not bear the penetration of his stare. "What?" I mumbled gracelessly.

"Will you allow me to carve her face? I have studied your methods these past days, and I believe my skill is equal to this."

What emotion did I feel then? Relief. Curiosity. Gratitude. Panic. All so crushed together I could not tell one from the other. He did not wait for me to answer. Placing his hands on my shoulders, he hoisted me from my position and steered me towards the mat where our meal was spread.

"Eat now," he said. "The rest of the work shall be mine."

I fought against my longing with no success. My resolve was insufficient for so great a task. The barricade I had built around my heart proved as flimsy and insubstantial as the mud-brick walls of a peasant's hut when struck by a freakish wave. For a while I occupied myself with the food before me, fixing my attention on the reed mat. But soon my eyes began to tire with the effort of keeping them there. They were drawn to Francisco and I had not the will to drag them away. Absorbed as he was with his task, he was unaware of my scrutiny. While I sat and stared, the dog Eve lay down next to me and placed her great head in my lap. My wariness of her had passed and I was stroking the wiry fur of her ears when Francisco at last looked up.

He said nothing, but lifted a hand and beckoned me to him. Awkwardly I rose. I could barely recall how to place one foot before the other as I crossed the tiles towards him. I stopped a short distance away, but he leant towards me, took my hand and pulled me down to look at what he had done.

When I saw what he had carved, I seemed to turn from solid flesh to molten gold. I had no form. No substance. I had dissolved; my soul had melted into his.

The face he had fashioned was my own.

He smoothed the waxen features with a single finger, and said in a voice so quiet that I had to bend my head to his, "I saw this girl when we first entered Tenochtitlán. It is to her I have given my heart. She stood on the causeway, struggling to contain her laughter. I would dearly love to see her smile like that again." Only then did he lift his eyes to mine. He traced the outline of my jaw. "My silent gold-smith," he whispered, lacing his fingers in my hair and pulling my face to his. "Did you think I would not know you?"

At the slap of a slave's feet on tiles we sprang apart guiltily. For what remained of the day we worked together in dizzying silence, smoothing wet clay over the surface of the statue until the face and form we had made was covered. It was then sundown, and in the dark we began to talk. At last I told him my name as we lay side by side. We did not touch, but my skin felt his nearness in every nerve. Bathed in moonlight, the air between us shimmered with desire.

"You gave no sign of recognition," I whispered. "Why did you say nothing?"

"In my own country, women do not dress as men. From what I have seen of this land, they do not do so here either. I thought you must have reason for such a disguise. I could not expose you."

"And yet you said nothing. Not even when we were alone."

"I have seen too many women forced into loving; I could not do such a thing! I wanted you to come willingly to me. Will you do so?"

"I cannot. Everything forbids it. The gods —"

"Must we speak of gods?" he sighed. "I struggle with the notion of paradise. It has no reality. Not when there is so much feeling here, now, on this earth."

His hands reached for mine and he pulled me towards him. I felt his mouth brushing my hair, my cheek, his hot breath on my neck. My skin touching his. Passion hung in the night air; I inhaled it until my chest ached. His heart beat hard against mine. I yielded.

We talked no more.

Had the sun lost its battle that night against the spirits of the underworld and failed to rise, I would have known neither fear nor anguish. Indeed, I prayed to all the gods that the concealing darkness would linger until our hunger for each other was satisfied. Yet dawn lightened the sky too soon, and the blast of the conch shells broke us apart.

The day was hot. By the time the sun was overhead, the clay had dried and was ready to be baked. When the wax had melted and trickled out, we began to cast our statue.

I paid little heed to the oddly shaped lumps of gold that Francisco set in the fire to melt. My attention was all on him, and on what we created. With great care we poured the molten metal into the mould, then waited anxiously for it to cool. Eagerly we broke the clay from the gold to reveal the finished statue beneath.

Cracking apart the mould covering her face, I started to throw the pieces aside. Francisco stopped me, opening my hands and examining the shards I held. Finding one that bore the imprint of the madonna's mouth, he took it and, binding it with twine, hung it about his neck.

"This I will keep," he said, lightly kissing my fingertips. "I will carry it with me always."

When the last of the clay was gone, we stood back to view the figure. It was perfect. But not until the sprues were removed, not until we had polished the whole to a dazzling shine, did I allow myself to take pride in what we had accomplished.

Then a triumphant smile split my face apart and I laughed. Not a giggle between clenched lips, stifled behind a hand for decency, but out loud with my head thrown back in exultation.

"There!" exclaimed Francisco. "That is the smile I have longed to see again!" And he reached out to embrace me.

But a voice knifed between us. "I see your work is done."

My father stood in the shadows, his face as dark as Mictlan. He had seen my unguarded smile. Heard my joyful laughter. If he had found me naked, entwined in Francisco's arms, it could not have told him more clearly what had passed between us.

22

"Axcahuah sent word that I was to come when I was recovered from my illness," my father said coldly. "He was troubled by the tardiness of my apprentice. And now I see the cause."

The look my father gave me then sliced my chest apart. I felt his hand reach inside and pull out my living heart. A daughter must do her father's bidding. I had dishonoured him. Shamed him beyond bearing. He said nothing more; he did not need to. Guilt drowned any words I could have offered in defence.

Axcahuah himself then came into the courtyard, bringing slaves to bear the statue to our emperor. His mind was too full of his own concerns to notice the tension between master and apprentice. The noble gave his orders. In strained silence we passed through the palace to the throne room.

I was startled by the change. Where once there had been veneration and servitude, now there was the noisy chatter of foreign tongues. And though my father and I bowed low and edged on our knees across the floor, Francisco remained upright, walking alongside us while we crawled like cockroaches towards the throne. I could see nothing, but from the babble that came from the dais I realized with some shock that the Spanish leader sat beside Montezuma, and it was the foreigner who approved the work we had done, giving a cry of pleasure when the figure of the golden madonna was unveiled.

We were rewarded as before with cloaks and cocoa, and dismissed.

I left that place walking next to my father, not behind him – his apprentice, not his invisible daughter. To survive we had to maintain this deceit. And yet how hard it was for me to hold my chin high. Shame dragged my eyes downwards and it was only with determination that I kept them looking ahead.

It took us some time to leave the palace, for a great many people were entering and we had to push against the tide of these new arrivals. I was so numbed with guilt and misery, I did not consider why such numbers of the elite – lords draped with golden bells, together with their richly ornamented wives and children – should be coming all at once to the emperor. Only later did I learn the reason. My sole concern then was what I would tell my father when we reached the privacy of our own home.

We did not know we were followed.

My father was so inflamed with anger that he did not glance behind. Only when we reached the doorway of our home did he stop, for Francisco had called out to him.

"Sir! My gracious and noble most esteemed lord chief emperor!" He rolled every courteous form of address he could muster into one ludicrous sentence. Francisco spoke my language well, but emotion – and fear of my father – rendered him inarticulate. Yet none could doubt the sincerity in his voice.

"Hear me. Please, I beg of you, let me speak."

My father turned to face him. He did not even look at me, but gave me a small push towards the house. "Get inside. Now. Before you are seen by our neighbours."

I did his bidding, running swiftly in. With haste I climbed to the roof, where I hoped to hear what was said. I was in time to see Francisco bow respectfully to my father.

He did his best, but he had few of the words he

needed to plead his case. Haltingly he said, "Your daughter … she is very…" He groped for a word, and could only find one that was used for fine feather wares. "She is very resplendent."

"Resplendent?"

Francisco tried again. "She is … golden."

"Golden?" If such a thing were possible, my father's voice grew colder still.

Francisco remained undaunted. "She is very valuable to me."

My father frowned. "To me also," he said. "Which is why I will protect her honour."

"Sir, I wish her no injury."

"I saw the look you gave her. You burn with desire!"

"Sir, believe me, I mean her no dishonour. I would like your daughter to be my…"

I prayed he would find the right word. But he had learnt our tongue from Tlaxcalan warriors. Soldiers. Slaves. He knew not the formal language of courtship. Of love. The word he finally used could not have been more wrong.

"Sir," he announced to my father and the whole listening neighbourhood, "I would wish your daughter to be my … my whore."

"Is that so?" My father's tone was calm. Dangerously so. He approached Francisco, arms outstretched as if to welcome him with an embrace. Francisco did likewise, a nervous smile flickering across his lips.

And then my father – master craftsman, man of peace – balled both hands into fists and struck Francisco in the belly so hard that he doubled over and fell to the ground. I gasped and turned, thinking to intervene. If I hastened down the steps I could stand between them. But Mayatl blocked my way, laying a restraining hand upon my arm.

"Leave them. You do enough damage returning home dressed as a youth! Let us hope no one has recognized you. Do not compound your foolishness by joining in with a brawl in the street. Change your clothes. Say nothing."

She had never spoken to me this angrily. And yet it was sound advice. I would do well to heed it. My father came in and went straight to his work-shop without a word; I knew better than to follow. Quietly I put on my women's clothes and went with Mayatl, working beside her all that day, and the many long days that followed. A frigid tranquillity descended upon our house. For, though I had saved him from the emperor's wrath and his certain death, my father could not bring himself to speak to me.

My father would not even allow me to venture as far as the market. I chained myself to the loom; there was nothing else I could do to occupy my hands and mind. There I proceeded to weave a cloth of such spectacular incompetence that Mayatl clucked her tongue in despair.

From her I learnt the news she had gleaned from the gossips in the square. We spoke softly lest we attract the disapproval of my father, but it was hard not to exclaim aloud when she told me of what had happened the day I returned from the palace.

I had seen the power the Spanish leader had over our emperor. And yet it seemed that Cortés himself was not content and wished to strengthen his grip upon our city further.

Montezuma had been compelled to summon all

the lords of the elite. I could confirm the truth of this rumour to Mayatl, for I had seen them gathering with my own eyes. They had been made to kneel before Cortés and swear loyalty to the Spanish throne.

To understand this ceremony was impossible. Mayatl and I tried, but could make no sense of such a thing. It was an incomprehensible ritual. There had been no war, nor had there been any declaration of one. None of the formalities necessary before a battle had been carried out. Montezuma would surely not allow it! And yet the rumour ran that Cortés had declared we were conquered; that this Spanish emperor whom we had never seen and could not even imagine was now our ruler!

"With no fight?" I exclaimed. "No bloodshed? How could we be defeated in such a way?"

It was so outrageously implausible that it should have been comical, and yet what Mayatl said next wiped any mirth from my mind.

The noblemen had been ordered to give over their wives and children into the keeping of the Spanish. It was a strange bondage, done under the guise of genial hospitality, yet no one could doubt that these innocents were prisoners within the palace, although they wore no chains. And when the families of our nobility had been taken, our emperor had made no sound of protest.

* * *

It was a time of uneasy, uncomfortable peace. It was accepted knowledge that Montezuma was hostage, not host, to the Spanish. And yet he was treated well by them. He went about the city in the company of their leader. The men I had seen cutting willows on the shore had fashioned them into pleasure boats in which Montezuma and Cortés could be seen bobbing upon the lake. They appeared to converse and exchange jests while the citizens of Tenochtitlán – who were no longer afraid to look upon the emperor's person – watched, sucking their teeth in disapproval.

But in all truth I must confess that I paid less heed to the manoeuvres of the great and powerful than I did to the silent conflict that raged in my own home.

My father moved about the house like a ghost. He watched me constantly, lest I try to slip away, but said nothing. He did not work, but instead sat, stiff with unspoken wretchedness. Even had he wished to craft anything, he could not. There was no gold to be had in Tlaltelolco. Anything of worth was in the hands of the Spanish leader.

My father's eyes had become deep, accusing pools. I hated to cause him so much anguish. Yet my remorse and regret were not equal to the desire I felt for Francisco. It ached in my throat; it tightened like a band across my chest, making each breath pained; it flamed within and could not be quenched. And though it cut my father to the quick, I could not let the matter rest, nor yield to his will without a fight.

When ten days had passed – days of such length they had seemed eternal – I took my courage in both hands and approached my father. In the courtyard where I had first scratched the image of Tezcatlipoca I bowed low, touching my forehead to the ground before my father as if he were the emperor.

"Forgive me, Father. I am sorry."

He grunted sceptically. "You are not. You burn for him. I see it in your eyes."

Carefully I answered, "I am sorry for the pain I cause you, Father. But you are right. I do not regret the time I spent in Francisco's company."

"I wish only to keep you safe," he said, shaking his head. "You see what these men are! And yet you throw yourself in the path of danger. What demon inspires you to such folly?"

"He has done me no harm."

"Itacate, he wants you for his whore!"

"He does not!"

"He said as much. Why else would I strike him?"

"He mistook the word, Father. He does not speak our tongue as well as he would wish."

"Itacate, you know what is done at the palace. You have seen it with your own eyes. The emperor is held there like an errant child. To buy the favour of his captors, our lord has given his women as gifts. His own nieces – his own daughters! You think they are there to roll tortillas?"

I lowered my head. I had seen how the strangers treated women, but knew Francisco was as repelled as I by their behaviour. "I can only say that this man is different from the others. He has not ill-treated me. And I—" A rising sob stoppered my throat. I could speak no more.

My father muttered bitterly, "I should have paid more heed to the priests at your birth. Had I kept you confined to the house, this would not have happened. I should never have let you cross the threshold of my workshop. Never put gold in your hands for you to fashion." Heaving a great sigh, he then spat vehemently, "The gods have taken one child from me. I will not let them take another! Daughter, do you not see the peril that shadows the path you tread? Do you willingly stride into disaster? These are our enemies, Itacate. You cannot mix with them without causing great harm to yourself. And if you will not consider yourself, think of those around you. Do you not see the damage you will do? You must forget him."

I made no reply. Crouching before me, my father put his hand under my chin and raised my face to his.

"I see in your eyes that you are not persuaded." He dropped his hand and looked up to the heavens. "The gods must be laughing at me. How have I offended them to get such a stubborn child?"

Softly I said, "When you first saw my mother —"

"Do not bring her into this!" The violence of his reaction shocked me and I drew back, flinching. "It is not the same," he said hotly.

My own temper rose to meet his. "It is."

"She was of my own city: my own race. By all the gods, I would rather give you as mistress to a Tlaxcalan than see you as whore to this heathen!"

"I cannot choose whom I love! You of all people should understand. It is not some cloth that I can fold and put away simply because you bid me to."

"This is mere fancy. You are a child, you do not know what you speak of."

"I am the age my mother was when you met her. She knew her own mind, did she not?"

My father paled. In a cracked whisper he said, "She did. And look what fate came to her." He was still for a moment, his face growing more gentle as he remembered. But then, recalling himself, he told me with renewed fervour, "You are to forget this man. I forbid you to see him. That is the end of it."

"I cannot."

"You must. You will. You are not to be seen in the company of a Spaniard! It will bring disaster to us all. It is my command."

I stood and faced him. I was chilled. Fearful. But I could say nothing else. "Then I must disobey you."

My father stared at me, disbelieving. Then, through clenched teeth, in a voice low with menace he spoke. "I have never struck you, child. Do not tempt me to do so now."

I matched his threat with one of my own. "You put aside your parents to follow your heart. Will you make me do the same?"

I had pushed him too far. My gentle father raised his arm and dealt me a blow across the face. Then he turned and went from the courtyard, walking away into the street. And I, shocked and heartsore, curled up in a corner of the empty workshop and wept.

24

Whether I truly would have had the courage to disobey my father, I do not know. Two days later, when I had scarce recovered from the shock of his blow, I heard a screaming cry in the street. It was answered by another, followed by a surge of panicked voices as neighbours stepped outside to see what was the cause.

I was trapped within my loom but Mayatl was on the rooftop tending to our hives. She called down to the people below, "What is the matter? What has happened?"

Several shouts came back.

"The gods!"

"They are stealing our gods!"

"From the temple!"

"They are taking our idols!"

Hearing these calls, my father hurried from his workshop towards me. "Do you know anything of this?" he asked.

Blankly I shook my head. "We did not speak of it."

Suddenly our own troubles were engulfed and rendered small and insignificant. The whole district was hastening to the temple precinct in blind terror; we were powerless to resist the flow. When my father stepped from the house he was swallowed up in the crowd. As soon as Mayatl had freed me from my loom we likewise joined the throng.

It was not the Spanish who took our gods away, but our own priests. The emperor gave the command but, with Cortés standing tall at his side, we knew who had placed the words in his mouth.

While we – a hushed, fearful assembly – fixed our terrified eyes on the principal temple at the heart of Tenochtitlán, the idols were removed. People paled at the sight, weeping softly, trembling, moaning and crying aloud to the gods for forgiveness. For this great act of sacrilege would undoubtedly bring punishment. Gently, carefully, with ropes and matting they were lowered down the stone steps. Huitzilopochtli, god of war. Tlaloc, who brings the rain. Tezcatlipoca.

The terracotta figure stared at me as it was laid, ungainly, on its side, and I stared back, mouth hanging open in wordless remorse.

The idols were carried away to secret places where I knew the priests would continue to let their own blood before them. How long this would keep the gods' wrath at bay, no one could tell. Some went swiftly to the other temples of the city to utter reverent prayers, for there were many altars in Tenochtitlán, many idols and many priests. Surely, people whispered to each other, while these remained, the sun could not be in danger?

I stood, unable to move, watching aghast as the temple steps were whitewashed. But the blood of ancient sacrifice could not so easily be wiped away, and it seeped through the white, staining it dull brown so that none could forget the temple's purpose.

The idols were gone. In their stead the foreigners placed their own gods. Black-skirted holy men bore figures towards the shrines: the man on the cross; the saint who carried a child upon his shoulder. And at their head – glinting on top of the temple pyramid for the whole city to see – was set the golden madonna.

She had seemed so large, so magnificent, in the palace courtyard. Up there she looked small. Unimpressive. Alien. She had no power in Tenochtitlán.

I was weak with shock at the insult given to our gods. Sick with the knowledge of what my own hands had done.

While I remained frozen and immobile, the Spanish holy men conducted their own ritual. Crossed wooden poles were erected at the foot of the temple steps, and before this the gathered soldiers knelt.

For a moment, my spirit leapt to see that Francisco was amongst them. He was so close! I fought the desperate longing to go to him. I could not! Not in the sunlit square. Not openly. Our desire, it seemed, was a shameful thing, fit only for the dark hours of night. Sensing my presence, he turned to look at me. Our eyes met, and I read in them both love and sadness. He glanced guiltily towards the golden madonna, and shame clenched my stomach in its cold fist so tightly that I covered my face and could not look at him again.

The Spanish holy men walked between the ranks, placing a morsel of food in each mouth, proffering each man a drink from a silver vessel. None in our city had ever seen such a ceremony, and there was much speculation as to its meaning. The words spoken were translated and whispered from mouth to mouth. It was said the strangers were eating the body of their god, and drinking his blood. Every brow was drawn into deep, perplexed furrows as we strove to comprehend the strange horror of this barbaric rite.

When they had finished, the Spanish force returned to the palace. They moved as one tightly pressed body and Francisco was carried with them, unable to break free. I watched as the great doors were shut between us. Only then could I find the strength to direct my feet homewards. I walked slowly, numb with misery. All about me, others did the same.

So deep was the city's distress, so many were the rumblings of profound unease, that the Spanish leader stayed his hand awhile. For the length of that day and the days that followed, Cortés left the city's many temples in peace. Impassioned prayers rang aloud from the tops of pyramids and much blood flowed as sacrifices were made to appease the deities we had so dishonoured.

Yet we waited for his next move, knowing some outrage would soon follow and that the gods we had offended would do nothing to save us. And all the while, the golden madonna glinted on the temple pyramid, a dreadful reminder of my own part in the catastrophe that was to come.

25

*T*ales hatched and bred as fast as flies in summer. It was said that Tezcatlipoca walked the city streets breathing fear into every heart. That Huitzilopochtli, god of war, had abandoned our warriors in favour of the Tlaxcalans. That Tlaloc would withhold the rains and make the harvest fail. We would go hungry. Thirsty. We would be enslaved. Slaughtered.

We would perish.

And then it was whispered that Cortés intended something more dreadful than anyone had dreamt of: he would put an end to sacrifice.

It was a neighbour who brought word of it to us, entering our house as we were beginning our noonday meal and casting his words upon the floor, where they thudded, heavy as stones. Mayatl's shock was so great that she dropped her vessel of crushed tomatoes, and a red stain spread across the tiles of our kitchen.

"It cannot be true!" protested my father. "He cannot do this!"

"And yet they say he will."

It was Mayatl who spoke the words that lay in all our hearts. "But how shall the sun rise?"

Our neighbour was unable to answer. He went on his way, spreading terror throughout our district until the air of Tlaltelolco was rank with it.

We finished our meal in silence, each of us knowing that we faced something worse than the end of our city, the end of our empire. We faced the end of the fifth age – the destruction of the earth itself.

And yet in the face of the cataclysm glimmered a small fragment of hope.

My father and I had not spoken of Mitotiqui since he had become the living god, for fear that Tezcatlipoca would hear and be angered. We did not breathe my brother's name now. And yet I knew what was in my father's mind when he called me to his workshop after our meal.

He had seen Mitotiqui's face when he was taken; he had understood its meaning as well as I. He too was haunted by his look. But if sacrifice were ended, Mitotiqui – unwilling as we thought he was – might be saved.

"Do you think there is truth in this last rumour?" he asked softly.

"Truly, I know nothing, Father. When I was at the palace we did not speak of this."

My father paced restlessly about the floor. He could not be still. Wringing his hands, he turned to me suddenly and said, "I must know. My curiosity writhes like a serpent within; it cannot be contained. I am loath for you to do it, but you have the means to find out. Tomorrow, at dawn, go to the palace. Find the youth of whom you are so fond. He alone can tell us what is to happen."

I slept little that night. Fear. Desire. Excitement. Dread. All spun in my mind like a whirlwind and would give me no rest.

In the darkness before dawn I dressed in the guise of a boy once more, for I dared not walk there in my own clothes. When the sun rose above the horizon, I slipped from the house.

I approached the palace, wondering how I would gain entry. But the guard who stood at the gates recognized me.

"Are you here again, boy? Did you leave something behind?"

"Yes," I replied with relief. "Some tools. May I collect them?"

At his command, the wooden barriers swung open and I walked inside.

I had only ever passed through the palace on the heels of Axcahuah. Without him to guide me it was harder to find the way, and I trod with nervous trepidation, trying to avoid the notice of the rowdy Spaniards. But at last I smelt the familiar scent of a charcoal burner. The tang of melting gold.

Stepping boldly now, I followed the smell until I came to the courtyard at the rear of the palace.

What I saw could not have shocked me more.

The courtyard was still filled with gold; strange solid slabs like the mud bricks of a farmer's hut were neatly stacked along one wall. But there were few fine ornaments, and what remained were heaped carelessly about the tiled floor. Some were broken into pieces. The gleaming jaguars that had reposed either side of the emperor's staircase were here, lying on their backs, their cleverly crafted feet clawing at the empty air. Their heads had been hacked off and their emerald eyes prised out, leaving dull, blind sockets. The silver monkeys dangled no more from their gleaming trees but were brought to ground as if by a violent earthquake.

And there, in the midst of this ruination, was Francisco! My heart rushed with joy to see him. But before I could move he stepped towards a statue. My figure of Tezcatlipoca! With the face of Francisco. Heart suddenly in my mouth, I looked to see if he recognized his own features.

He showed no expression. Puzzled, I froze in the shadows to see what he would do.

He caressed the figure. Ran his fingers over it. Then he took a knife and prised the obsidian from the hand of the god, cracking the stone and throwing it aside as if it had no value. He pushed my statue to the floor. Took a hammer. Pounded it flat. Broke it into shards. Set them in the fire.

Aghast, lifting my hands to my cheeks, I swayed with consternation. Rage swept through me and a scream of unspeakable anger rose in my throat as I leapt forward to stop this wanton destruction.

Francisco turned and saw me, and at once a delighted smile split his face. But, seeing the fury in my eyes and hearing the shout that burst from my lips, he seized me, clasping a hand tightly over my mouth. Snaking an arm about my waist, he carried me swiftly from the courtyard, through the slaves' quarters and into the narrow alley beyond.

Once there he released me, but not before he had muttered urgently in my ear, "Do not scream. Say nothing. If the other men see you, you are lost. Believe me, Itacate, I do not want you discovered."

I did not cry out. But my heart pounded against

226

my chest with rage. "What were you doing?" I asked in a harsh whisper. "To destroy such things! It is barbaric. Why would you wish it?"

He put a hand to his brow and rubbed between his temples. Wearily, in a voice drained of passion, he said only, "I do as I am bid."

"To crush such artistry!"

"I do not like my work, Itacate. I did not seek it."

"What kind of villain follows such orders?"

"One who wishes to live."

His tone silenced me. He made no apologies. No excuses. Yet my statue was gone! Despair washed over me and I wept.

"They are objects, Itacate. Lifeless objects. Do they matter so much?"

"You know they do," I answered. "Spoil the work and you slay the maker." Wiping the tears from my face, I lifted my chin and glared at him. "That was my statue."

"You crafted it?" Pain furrowed Francisco's brow. "Oh, dear god!"

"Why does your leader ruin things of such beauty? Has he no soul?"

"He has not." When it came, Francisco's voice was as anguished as my own. "He does not see artistry; he sees only wealth. Gold cannot be valued unless it is weighed. It cannot be weighed with accuracy unless it is in blocks. So he commands me to melt it all."

"All?" I echoed, recalling the strangely shaped pieces he had placed in the fire when we had cast the virgin in gold. Chilled with sudden dread, I asked, "Was the madonna made from the destruction of such treasures?"

Francisco did not speak, but I saw the answer in his eyes. Sighing sadly, he took my limp, unresisting hand in his. "We were cast from the same mould, you and I. Believe me, I know the worth of these pieces. I feel their skill here, in my heart. You think I would put them in the fire if I had a choice?"

"Is he so harsh, then, your leader? Even to those who follow him?"

"He is brutal. To those who do not do his bidding, his punishments are extreme. And I ... Itacate, I cannot live without my hands."

I struggled to divine his meaning. "He would sever them?"

Francisco nodded, his face twisted with pain. And yet I could not believe him. No leader would do such a thing. To remove a man's hands and compel him still to live? It was impossible! He had invented this lie so that I should forgive him. But I could not.

"You say Cortés is cruel, yet I see none of it.

228

You lie. You do what he tells you because you are a coward!"

I pulled away from him, wresting my hand from his so violently that my skin was pinched and bruised. I turned and fled, hot tears spilling down my cheeks. At that moment, Francisco's name was shouted within the palace, but he did not go at once to his masters. He called after me, his voice pleading, desperate, but I did not stop. And so Francisco returned to his destruction, and I – still ignorant of the fate that would befall my brother – returned home.

*T*he doubts I held as to the unnatural cruelty of the Spanish leader were soon dispelled.

Perhaps a month after I had fled from Francisco, an event took place in the temple precinct that made me see the truth of all he had told me and understand the perilous position he was in.

Some days before, Cortés had sent his messengers from our city to the coast. They had been slain as they journeyed. Montezuma had called for Qualpopoca, the leader of the town where it had happened, to come to Tenochtitlán.

In good faith Qualpopoca obeyed, bringing with him his sons and nobles, for they trusted our lord emperor. They were of the elite; they had neither lifted the knives themselves, nor knew who was responsible. Indeed, some in our city muttered that a god had done the killing for it was well known that the Spanish had desecrated a temple in the town and stolen the golden idols from its altar.

The nobles were betrayed.

Our emperor ordered that they be punished, although all could hear the Spanish leader's voice in the words he chose.

I heard the proclamation in the marketplace; since I had returned from the palace so violently angered against Francisco, my father's own fury had softened and I was once more free to walk the city streets. Scarce believing the evidence of my own ears, I went to the temple precinct, falling in with a crowd of baffled onlookers.

The centre of the square was empty, save for several large piles of fresh-cut willow from which tall poles protruded skywards. I pushed my way to the front of the crowd to better see but was only puzzled further by the broken spears and cudgels which had been added to the green wood. It seemed the Spanish had taken the weapons from our warriors' armoury.

The makeshift doors of the palace swung open, and from there our emperor came. No one lowered their heads. No one averted their eyes. All saw him following behind Cortés like a faithful dog.

A dais had been erected, and climbing onto this the two leaders could be seen clearly by those assembled in the square. They were at once surrounded by Spanish soldiers, well armed with what we now knew to be guns and crossbows. Then came the rest of their force, assembling in rigidly straight lines along the length of the palace walls. Francisco was amongst them. I saw him a moment before he laid his eyes on me; before he stepped forward as though to call my name, and received a sharp jab with the end of a spear for stepping out of his allotted place. He made no further move. Enraged though I still was, I felt the awareness hanging between us, tying us together with a silken thread. Through all the dreadful spectacle that followed, I felt its tug.

Raising his arms aloft, the emperor spoke the words he was commanded to. With no tremble in his voice, sounding as though all feeling had died with his captivity, he declared, "For crimes against our honoured guests, these nobles shall be punished. The sentence is death."

An astonished cry leapt from every mouth. Death? It was unjust! The hands of the Spanish soldiers went at once to their weapons, and this was enough to still the audible stirrings of discontent. When all fell silent, the Spanish leader gave a signal, and those who were to die were led in chains towards the piles of wood. Roughly they were forced to climb on, and were tied to the upright poles. Never had we seen such a punishment. No one could imagine what was to come next. I looked to Francisco, but his head was lowered, his whole body seeming crushed with the weight of despair.

It was then that a Spanish holy man came forth. To each of the nobles he went, offering them the touch of the large black book he carried. His words were loudly translated so we all understood he was promising the men salvation: if they would convert to the Spanish faith they would live for ever in paradise.

One asked if there would be Spaniards in this heaven. When he was given the answer yes, he turned his head away. "I will not spend eternity with savages."

The priest moved on to Qualpopoca. The book, he told him, spoke the word of god. Qualpopoca inclined his head, frowning with concentration as if trying to hear its voice. But at last he raised his chin proudly and spoke. In the hushed square his words rang loud. "I hear nothing. Your book does not speak to me." And then he spat in contempt. I was far from him, but I could imagine the spittle hitting the leather volume, balling and rolling slowly down its cover.

The holy man gave a furious shriek. Skirts flying, he ran towards a soldier who held a flaming torch. Wresting it from his hands, the priest took it and plunged it into the heap of wood.

It was not merciful, nor was it swift. Fresh willow is slow to burn. With neither pulque nor mushrooms to ease their passage, these nobles met their flaming deaths in screaming, ghastly anguish.

The horror, the imaginative cruelty of the punishment, reduced all those watching to silence. We had never seen the like. No one had ever dreamt that such a thing was possible.

Our emperor watched them burn, tears streaming down his face as the fetid air of the temple precinct turned black with smoke. When it was done, he was led away. Helpless. Weak. Lost. And as he climbed down from the dais, I saw his ankles were chained.

I did not look at Francisco. I did not even glance in his direction. But when the sickened crowds had melted away to their homes, and the Spanish had withdrawn to the palace, we two were left standing in the square.

I recall neither moving towards him nor reaching out. All I remember is the aching sorrow, the searing pain, as we stood holding each other. Not caring who saw us, disregarding the censure we would bring down on our heads, we clung to one another as tightly as drowning fishermen to a canoe. But though we tried to keep our heads aloft, we knew we were in grave danger of slipping beneath the dark waters of despair.

A week after the burnings, Francisco managed to break free from the palace and ventured once more to our home, standing humbly in the street until he was given permission to enter. Despite the danger that followed on his heels along with the dog Eve, his constant companion, my father did not turn him away. Francisco alone could give him knowledge of what might happen to my brother. Though he asked not of Mitotiqui, my father longed to have some insight into what lay in the Spanish leader's mind.

The air of Tenochtitlán had grown thick with anticipation of dreadful events to come. As winter had turned to spring, people scurried about the streets like birds, darting from building to building as though a mighty jaguar stood in the shadows ready to pounce. A dark current whirled beneath the lake, threatening to pull our floating city down to some unknown place. There was a restless edge. A breath of violent menace that would erupt at the slightest provocation.

The Spanish leader held the emperor and thus he held the city. Or so he thought. He could not know that with each day Montezuma spent at Cortés's side, the power to influence his people was waning. The foreign force had eaten its way through the maize stored in vast chambers as protection against future famine. And now there were mutterings that, if a provincial nobleman like Qualpopoca could find the courage to spit upon a Spaniard before he burned, our own leader should find the courage to do the same before the population starved. There were rumblings of discontent. Murmurings of anger. The talk on the streets was all of change. Something would happen; something would break this brittle calm. But whether it would be in our favour or theirs was impossible to say.

And to this general unease was added the particular dread of what would become of my brother.

My father sat with Francisco in his workshop. It was a strange, awkward meeting. I knelt between them, and though I hoped for a mutual liking to grow, there was none. My father was rigid with anxiety for my brother, and Francisco could do little to comfort him. "It is true Cortés wishes to put an end to sacrifice," he said. "He has spoken of it often. And yet he does nothing."

"Why does he wish to stop it?" asked my father.

Francisco grimaced. "Because it gives his expedition moral purpose," he replied. "Cortés can justify any act, any brutality, as long as he says he does it for our god. For the true faith. Our priests will then forgive him anything. As will our own emperor. But whether he will dare to, I cannot say."

"Does your leader not tell you what he plans?" snapped my father.

"Does yours tell you?" countered Francisco. "Cortés is wilful. Capricious. We are here not because of some carefully ordered scheme, but because he is a gambler. An opportunist. Gold is the one god he worships. None of us can say what he will do next."

"The spring festival is almost upon us," my father said quietly.

I felt Francisco stiffen beside me. He turned his face to mine, his brows arched in a question. "Did you not once tell me that your brother—"

"—is the living god," I interrupted. "Yes. It is a great honour for our family. You know a little of the ceremony, I think? A *willing* sacrifice goes to glory on the festival's fourth day."

If Tezcatlipoca was listening, my words could not offend him. But my eyes told Francisco a different tale. They confirmed what he had once guessed for himself.

He looked slowly from me to my father. "Then I must warn you that our holy men urge Cortés to stop the ritual. They insist upon it. But he fears the city will rise up against him. We are well weaponed, but we are fewer in number. I do not know what will happen. I cannot tell you more. I am sorry."

My father gave him a brief nod in response and withdrew, leaving the house once more to pace the city streets. We were left alone, and for a time we lost ourselves in each other, stealing joy amidst the devastation that swirled about us.

Too soon, Francisco had to return to the palace. Holding me close, he said in a soft whisper that surely no god could hear, "I do not know if there is anything that can be done to save your brother. But if there is … I must be certain: do you wish me to do it?"

We stood, foreheads pressed together. The smallest movement of my head gave my assent. I made no other reply. There was nothing more that could be said. We both knew that the people of Tenochtitlán would not allow the sun to perish. If Cortés – if Francisco – dared to make this move against our faith, the city would be provoked into war.

It was on a day of sweet spring sunshine that disaster finally came to Tenochtitlán. Despite the tension and fear of trouble, the people sang as they went about their business, for the festival of Toxcatl was upon us. Four days of feasting and dancing in honour of Tezcatlipoca. Four days of processions and rituals with their beautiful, haunting power.

And at the end, my brother would die. On the fourth day, Mitotiqui would enter paradise.

Or he would not.

If his death dishonoured the god, he would walk for ever in the gloom of Mictlan.

I was tormented by the suspicion that he had lied: that he had never seen the god; that his rash words had been born of jealousy. And without his joyful willingness, what was left?

Death.

Ugly. Futile. Cruel.

I was in agony as the festival began. My father stood beside me in the crowd, and I could feel him tremble as we watched.

A fanfare. The beat of many drums. And then there, on the steps of the great temple, stood

Mitotiqui, dressed in the robes of a warrior. My brother, my twin, one half of my soul. Looking at his familiar face after so long made sweet memories of childhood flood my mind and brought bitter tears to my eyes.

Four women – great beauties – were given to him. They would be his companions during his last days and nights on earth. Before he descended the steps, my brother surveyed the city square below him. He did not look at me, but as his eyes slid over the assembled worshippers I saw that no blinding glory lit him from within. The god did not possess him. His eyes were dulled with pulque, and for that I was grateful. If I too could have deadened my senses and blurred my mind, I would have drunk myself into oblivion.

Mitotiqui climbed into a litter; he was hoisted high and then carried through the city at the head of an exultant procession. Flowers were strewn in his path. People fell on their knees before him. Men begged to be blessed with a touch of his fingers; women fainted in the crush that surrounded him. And my father and I followed, dazed, and sick with sorrow.

For three days the festival escalated in intensity. Dancing at sacred sites grew more frequent and the participants more numerous, until it seemed as though the whole city throbbed with the beat of one drum and all paced the elaborate steps of a ritual dance.

I had to watch it all; had to feast and worship with a smile fixed on my lips. But my heart lay dead inside me. I knew well that I should not feel as I did. If Tezcatlipoca looked into his smoking mirror and saw what lay in my mind, he would be outraged. Who knew what the result would be if that happened? I did not want to bring his wrath upon my city. And yet I could not shape my thoughts and feelings to what they should be.

I was tense beyond bearing, my nerves pulled tight as the threads of my loom. There was a dreadful foreboding in the air; a sense of calamity to come.

On the fourth day, the frenzied drumming, the wailing chants, rose to a crescendo. And on this day, fear of the Spaniards' ill intent reached its zenith.

It was my brother's day of death. The day he would be released from the illusion we call life, and pass through to the greater reality.

The temple precinct was filled with many thousands of people. An intense religious fervour gripped the city, magnified by the horror of the sacrileges we had been forced to commit. Every heart beat with repentance. Every eye streamed with tears. Every mouth pleaded for forgiveness. Our idols had been removed from the great temple pyramid, but for the duration of the spring rites so had the Spanish gods. The golden madonna was hidden, and in her place stood a grimacing effigy of Tezcatlipoca which had been fashioned for his festival.

Dancers spun and whirled across the square in richly embroidered loincloths, over which hung cloaks woven with fur and feathers. The spotted skins of animals were worn in strips around their ankles, and their bodies were draped with strings of shells. Golden lip plugs and earrings pierced their flesh, and tiny golden bells – all of which had miraculously escaped the attentions of the Spanish – tinkled as they swayed, a sweet sound that was at odds with the expression of intense concentration etched across the brow of every dancer.

My father and I were carried in a litter through the crowd that comprised every soul in the city. When we reached the temple, we were lifted onto the dais from which we were to watch. This sacrifice brought great distinction to our family; thus my father and I were compelled to stand raised up before the onlookers so that all could see how we gloried in this rite.

Dread wrapped itself around me like a sodden cloak, but I could not let go the tiny splinter of hope with which Francisco had pierced my heart.

From where I stood, I could see Spanish soldiers threading through the crowd. Sunlight glinted on plumed helmets, on armoured breastplates, on polished swords. There was their leader, flanked by his holy men.

The dance ended. There was a silence, which was broken by the shouts of Spanish priests urging Cortés to act.

The crowd parted, and Mitotiqui – painted the blue of sacrifice – walked alone across the square. A great scream was rising within me. A cry of rage, a desolate howl, that I could scarcely contain.

The presence of Tezcatlipoca was palpable. I had felt him walk the city streets and dance amongst the men. He had sat beside me, crushing me, as I was carried in the litter. Now his cool fingers traced the bones of my spine. His chill breath was on my neck as Mitotiqui's hair was cut. My brother stood a spear's length from me. So close! I could push my way through to him. Take his hand and tug. We could run to the chinampa fields. To freedom.

But we were children no longer.

A sigh of expectation ran through the crowd like a breath of wind rippling the surface of the lake.

Mitotiqui was handed a flute. A conch. Raising them above his head, he mounted the first of the temple steps. Turning to face the crowd, he lifted his hand in a gesture of farewell.

As he looked about him for the last time, his eyes met mine and I had to bite my lip to stop the scream from bursting forth. For at that moment I saw not the dulled, dead eyes of one whose mind was fixed on paradise, but the eyes of a boy. The eyes of my brother. Full of pain. Misery. Anguish.

Mitotiqui was terrified.

The scream rose; my chest ached with holding it. I swallowed, over and over again, for a rock had lodged itself hard in my throat. My mouth ran dry and my tongue seemed to swell until it choked me. I could not breathe. The priests' eyes were on me. Peeling back the skin. Seeing the truth in my heart. I had to keep silent; mask my distress. My heart sounded like the clanging of a great bell, and my whole body trembled with its reverberation. My breath came in gasps. My palms were cold. Clammy. I was shivering. Clenching my teeth to stop them chattering.

Mitotiqui turned to face the steps.

A Spanish cry. A shouted command.

My brother began his ascent.

Spanish soldiers pushed through the throng.

Mitotiqui reached the top.

The press of people was too great. The soldiers could not get through.

Mitotiqui broke his flute.

Swords unsheathed.

Arms outstretched, my brother submitted himself to the priests.

Golden curls near the temple. A youth breaking free.

Mitotiqui on the altar.

Francisco running up the steps.

The priest's knife raised aloft. Black obsidian, glinting in the sun.

Francisco's sword drawn.

The crowd took a sharp breath; thousands of mouths drew in air at the selfsame moment. There was none left for me. It was sucked from my lungs, squeezed from my body. In that dreadful, airless pause, I prayed that time would freeze. Go backwards. Cease.

Francisco's yell.

My brother's scream.

The knife came down.

As Francisco reached the top of the temple steps, my brother's blood flowed to meet him.

28

When the flute of the new Tezcatlipoca rang across the square, the dancing began once more. I was scarcely aware of the soldiers who made their way between the onlookers.

Numb with grief, I knew only that Francisco was suddenly at my side, tugging me from the dais. Eve was yelping anxiously, almost drowning out his words.

"You must move, Itacate. Leave now. Cortés's mood is ugly. It is not safe here."

I could not set one foot in front of the other. Horror held me to the spot. My eyes were fixed on Francisco's boots, soaked with my brother's blood. A low moan – the cry of an injured animal – escaped me, a noise that I barely recognized as coming from myself.

"He is dead!" I sobbed. "He is gone!" Dragging

my eyes to Francisco's face, I accused him. "You were too slow."

Francisco was stricken. "We were not meant to succeed. Cortés's command came too late. Our priests are appeased by this sham of action; now they will forgive him anything. You do not know what my comrades can do. For god's sake come away from this place!"

His desperate plea could not be resisted. He half dragged, half carried me across the square, yelling at my father to follow.

The dancers spun, and the beat of the drums became louder, more insistent. The men of Tenochtitlán sang, lifting their hearts and voices to the heavens, begging the god for peace, for children, for health, for wisdom. Feet pounded the stone slabs in ever more rapid steps. Sweat filled the air with a salty tang. They were blind with ecstasy. They did not see they were surrounded.

Steel glinted in the sun. The soldiers' swords were raised. Perhaps even then, they might not have attacked.

But as Francisco dragged me through the press of people, I saw the wizened man with jaguar-clawed feet approach the Spanish leader. Titlacuan, the destroyer. His eyes flared with divine possession. He lifted his stick and struck Cortés across the face.

One shout. That was all it took for the slaughter to begin. Incensed, the Spaniard yelled aloud in his rage and the soldiers fell upon the dancers.

Hands were hacked off, heads severed, stomachs slashed open. The murder of these unarmed men took no time at all. But the Spanish were not content with these lives alone. They turned upon the crowd, slicing those red-bladed swords through garlanded girls, plump-limbed boys, mothers with babies in their arms.

Some ran to the temple, attempting to evade their attackers by climbing the steps. They were pursued and the whitewashed stones were drenched anew with scarlet. The air was thick with the stench of blood, clogged with the screams of the dying. And still Francisco pulled me away.

We had reached the canal, were about to cross the bridge, when our path was blocked. A warrior – a man of my own race – gave a violent cry. Stepping forward, he swung his cudgel at Francisco's head. The obsidian blades bit deep, cutting through his ear and sinking into his jaw.

It can have lasted no longer than a heartbeat, but that moment seemed to stretch into eternity. Francisco's eyes sought mine. He opened his mouth to speak, but only blood spilled from between his lips. And then his lake-blue eyes glazed to grey. Without a word, Francisco fell, his face smashing onto the stone street. I made no sound. My mind could not accept what my eyes had seen, and disbelief robbed me of my voice. Only Eve told of her misery. Standing astride Francisco's unmoving body, she raised her head and howled.

I did not stay with him. Though I resisted, my father had seized my arm and was dragging me from there when the fleeing crowd burst from the square behind us, running in terrified panic. We were carried with them.

Later, much later, we sat in our home too grieved for talk, too horrified for thought. All was cold and bleak and comfortless.

Then I heard a single bark and ran into the street. For a fleeting moment, I thought he was with her. That he had somehow escaped the slaughter. He had come to me!

But Eve was alone, and I knew then that Francisco's death was certain.

29

*I*t was war. Pure. Simple.

The Spanish leader had mesmerized our emperor;
held him bewitched and the city enthralled. But now
the spell was broken. The warriors had awoken.
Death stalked the city.

The Spanish force and their Tlaxcalan followers had retreated into the palace. At first light our
own warriors gathered outside the walls, armed
with new-made cudgels and lances. A crowd gathered on the temple steps to watch our men take their
revenge. I too was drawn there, compelled by the
god to witness it. I stood close to the palace, for I
cared nothing for my own safety.

There were shouts and cries, and our warriors
fought savagely and with relish. But with no leaders – for they lay amongst the slain – there was no

251

one to direct the attack. As I watched, a small group banded together and attempted to scale the walls. A makeshift ladder was leant against the palace, and a jaguar warrior swiftly ascended with the speed of a monkey. He reached the flat roof, but before he could set foot on it, a soldier appeared, sword slashing. From the precinct below, an arrow was sent thudding into the chest of the Spaniard and he fell, plunging headfirst onto the stone. Those standing on the temple steps sent up a great cheer.

The warrior was on the roof, raising his cudgel, striking at the swarm of soldiers who came to fight. He was stopped by the smoking shot from a Spanish gun and sent hurtling to the ground, landing lifeless on the stone as the soldier had done. The ladder was pushed away, crashing down on our men below. They stood in groups, debating what their next move should be.

But they were in no hurry. The Spaniards were trapped and outnumbered. Our warriors would find a way to penetrate the palace and then our enemy would die – of that there could be no doubt.

Close as I was to the palace walls, I heard the commotion within before the massed warriors did. A Spaniard – his voice so angry that it carried clearly through the upper-floor windows – was calling our emperor's name and shrieking, "Look! I am wounded! See what your men have done to me!"

The words were translated for our emperor, and then I heard his clear reply.

His voice seemed to contain every sorrow in the city. With immense dignity he said, "Cortés, my friend, if you had not begun it, my men would have no need to finish it this way. You have ruined yourself, and me also."

His reply caused even greater fury to erupt in the Spaniard. I heard sounds of struggle, a cry of protest, and then the emperor was forced onto the roof. I moved back to better see what took place, but the crowd closed so hard about me that I could not. Sunlight dazzled my eyes, but I beheld Montezuma, lord of the world, outlined against the sky as he was forced to address his warriors.

"Put down your shields; unstring your bows. We must have no more of this battle. My children, our dead are many. The sacred rites must be observed if their souls are to enter paradise. For the sake of our loved ones, go now. Go home and mourn them."

His plea was eloquent. It touched the hearts of all those who heard it. And, to honour the dead, his people did as they were asked. For if they were not given all due ceremony, the souls of our loved ones would be lost and wandering for eternity. All went home to grieve their losses, and the Spanish were left in peace. And I – fearing my brother's soul was in Mictlan, knowing Francisco's heathen spirit was condemned to roam this earth without rest – could pray to our angered gods for neither.

For many days, wakes and funerals dominated the city. The elite were buried, the commoners burned. The Spanish had slaughtered the flower of our nobility: artisans, craftsmen, peasants alike. The smoke of many thousands of cremations hung like a cloud above Tenochtitlán. The sound of fathers sobbing, widows wailing and mothers weeping echoed through the empty streets and was carried across the still lake until the mountains themselves seemed to cry in loud lament.

30

*G*rief. Fear. They wear the same mask. Both gnaw at the insides and give no rest. In those days an ominous calm held Tenochtitlán frozen, and yet I seemed beset with parasites that wormed and tunnelled through the very marrow of my bones. I itched with an intolerable restlessness; I could not keep still. Yet neither could I move about the city streets. My father begged me to keep within the house.

We were then in the time of Etzalcualiztli, the peak of the season of dryness. Food was often scarce at this time of year and, since the Tlaxcalan hordes had eaten our food reserves, many went hungry.

The priests had control of the city. They roamed wild and fearsome, insulting or beating anyone who displeased them, for they had to do whatever was necessary to bring the rains. They could take whomever they pleased for sacrifice: captives, slaves, children. Their hearts were then thrown into Pantitlan, the whirlpool that spun in the centre of the lake, in offering to Tlaloc.

When Mitotiqui and I were small, we had been confined to the rear of the house until the rains came lest we should attract the attention of a wandering priest. Now my father and Mayatl and I did the same. They had never been known to take grown citizens, but this was a time without precedent. We lived by eating what little remained growing in our roof garden. None of us ventured out.

During these days, I mourned for my brother. For Francisco. I could scarce take in all I had witnessed. While it was light I occupied my hands with grinding such corn as we had stored. It was a task I had once so despised, yet now it gave me something of a purpose and I was glad of it. Our meals were sparse, but our appetites were so dulled with unhappiness that we did not crave for more. While I rolled tortillas, and stuffed them with thin shreds of vegetable, my numbed mind refused to accept what had befallen those I loved. But in the darkness of night, truth pierced me like a knife. Paroxysms of grief convulsed me and I clung to Eve for comfort.

❊ ❊ ❊

While I was thus paralysed with sorrow, the men of Tenochtitlán were creating for themselves a new order. Our city was governed so tightly that we had no means or system for a single man to rise above his fellows and take command of them. But now necessity forged a different path. In the days when the city wept for its dead, the warriors formed a new hierarchy. With what rites and secret ceremonies the elite stripped power from Montezuma and made his brother Cuitlahuac emperor, I did not know. But Tenochtitlán had a new leader. One, moreover, who was intent on revenge.

Perhaps Cortés thought all resistance had ceased when the warriors were ordered home and that they would fight no more. Perhaps he could not bear to leave the city he had travelled so far to conquer, for he did not move from the palace.

When the days of ritual mourning were done, when the rains had come and the time of Etzalcualiztli was ended, our warriors struck. One night I awoke suddenly to the stench of burning. Climbing to the roof, I saw fires in the distance. Many flames pierced the darkness. I knew my city well and did not need to be told where these fires burned. The bridges. The pleasure boats the Spanish used to sail upon the lake. Torches had been put to them all. There would be no escape for our enemy.

As conch blasts called forth the dawn, the palace was surrounded by warriors: men dressed in the furs of leopards, or wearing the masks of eagles. Standing high on the temple steps beside my father, I saw it all and yet felt nothing. My body lived, but I was dead within.

For five days, there was fighting. Battle sounds rang in the square. Steel on wood. Roars of angry men.

On the afternoon of the sixth day, the Spanish leader was roused to desperate action. It had worked before. Our emperor had been forced onto the roof and the warriors had melted away.

And so Montezuma – shrunken with misery, unwashed, his face bloated with weeping – was once more paraded before us.

He could not have commanded a dog.

He raised his slackly withered arms above his head. Not one word fell from his mouth. Not one word reached the ears of the gathered crowd. A storm of stones, sticks, broken vessels – anything that came to hand – rained upon him. Pelted with missiles, pierced by shards of obsidian, bruised and bleeding, he was forced back within.

Whether he truly died of these wounds, I do not know. It was said by the Spanish that his own people had killed him. But a different tale was passed from mouth to mouth in Tenochtitlán.

Montezuma was of no further use to Cortés. Attacked by his own warriors, all authority gone, what purpose was there in keeping him alive? Like a toothless dog, he was nothing but an encumbrance. And so he suffered the same fate as a beast that has outlived its usefulness. He was slain. His attendants were slain with him. And the nobles' wives and children who had long ago been taken captive were slaughtered like animals, their bodies hurled from the palace roof into the precinct below.

It did not take long for word to travel. In the gathering dark the square was lit as bright as day by the flaming torches and braziers carried by the people of Tenochtitlán. They came for their husbands. Their brothers. Their sons. Wives. Sisters. Daughters. Throwing themselves on their corpses with wails of despair, their lamentations rang to the heavens. The buildings quaked with their suffering. The desolation I felt within was manifest all around me.

As I stood and watched the broken body of our emperor being carried from that place, I wept for him. For Mitotiqui. For Francisco.

For us all.

It was the god who woke me. Tezcatlipoca who breathed an icy chill through my bedchamber and caressed my flesh with his cold fingers. In the darkest hour of that night, he whispered in my ear.

I did his bidding.

I went to the palace.

The streets are deserted when dark, for it is a time of dread. The sun battles in the underworld, and who knows if it will win its fight and rise once more? In the night demons are abroad, and the gods are at their most fearsome: they wear the aspects of their dark sides and will violate and murder any who cross their path.

It was with trepidation that I set forth, barefoot so I would make no noise. Eve walked beside me, her claws clacking on the stones, the sound magnified in the still blackness. A fine drizzle streamed steadily from the sky, obscuring the brightness of the moon.

On nearing the palace, I was surprised to hear movement. At this late hour there should be nothing but Eve's paws and my own breathing. Yet now, whispered though they were, I caught hurried conversations, urgent commands, desperate questions.

The doors to the palace were wide open.

I shrank back into the shadows to watch. A horse was led forth, heavily laden. What it bore on its back was ill packed and poorly tied as though done in great haste. Through the gaps in the cloth I could see the glint of gold.

Gold. The metal that had drawn them here. The metal that – though their lives were in peril – they would not leave without.

For they were leaving, of that there could be no doubt. The first horse was followed by a line of men. Then more horses, their hooves bound in cloth to muffle their sound. The dogs' jaws were tied to prevent their barking, and some men walked barefoot as I did to avoid detection.

How different a procession it was to the one I had watched in awe just a few months ago! Then they had arrived with jangling armour, splendid and shining, like gods. Now they left like thieves. Cowards. Fleeing furtively from the city whose wealth they had plundered. Whose people they had slaughtered. Whose ruler they had destroyed.

They should not go unpunished.

I would give our people warning. Rouse the warriors. A yell erupted from my breast. "They are running away! Come quickly!"

At my sudden shout, the soldiers turned. One ran, sword drawn, to stop my noise. I did not move. As he came, I continued to cry aloud.

"They are fleeing the city! The Spanish are escaping!"

He raised his sword high as Eve barked a warning. But before he could reach me, people from nearby houses spilt into the square. Seeing them, the Spaniard turned and fled.

And now my shouts were taken up by others and carried to the temple. A drumbeat pounded from the top of the pyramid, waking all who still lay sleeping. Men and women tumbled through the doors of every house, and soon their running feet slapped loudly on the streets. Canoes glided swiftly through the canals towards the causeway. Many torches lit the night sky as brightly as the burning flame had done so long ago. Shouts of men – the warlike howls of warriors – rent the air.

With this, every trace of discipline in the Spanish force crumbled. Bearing planks of wood they had ripped from the palace, they attempted to make bridges on the causeway across which they could pass. Had they not been observed, they might perhaps have succeeded and made an orderly retreat. But thrown into panic and confusion as they were, all was chaos.

Those at the rear hastened forward, desperate to escape the onslaught of our warriors. They did not know – they could not – that the weight of their numbers forced those ahead into the canal before the planks could be laid down.

Men fell into the water and were drowned, dragged to the lake floor by the gold they had stuffed into their tunics. Horses, heavily laden with the stolen blocks of metal, screamed in terror before they too were pulled beneath the water. Others were pushed from the causeway as fear made men cruel. Tlaxcalan warriors. Tlaxcalan courtesans. Their bodies made the first bridge the Spanish stumbled across.

The causeway was long with many burnt bridges to cross before they reached solid land. They fled heedless of others, each man caring only to save his own skin. And as they fled, our canoes came at them from both sides. The sky rained arrows.

❊ ❊ ❊

Three quarters of the Spanish force was lost that night. In the cold grey light of the following dawn their bodies choked the clear lake, hanging in the water like a frenzied, monumental offering to the god Tlaloc.

Their leaving had been hastily arranged, so suddenly done that those who were lodged in the slaves' quarters had not heard word of it. Some hundred men had been left behind. Their capture took little effort on the part of our warriors. They were made to dance, naked, on top of the city's principal temple before their sacrifice. And with no mushrooms to dull the senses, their screams were loud and dreadful.

As I dressed in crisp, clean clothing, the ancient steps ran red with Spanish blood.

*T*he Spanish were gone. But the bloodlust they had roused did not go with them. It had to vent itself on someone. Lacking an enemy, the warriors turned their fury on our own people. To those who had aided our enemy – however unwillingly – they were without mercy.

I did not know such things were happening, or I should have made efforts to keep my father in our home. But I was in a kind of stupor, my mind deadened with misery, my senses clouded with sadness. Attempting to comfort me, my father had sent Mayatl to market to buy titbits with which to tempt my appetite, for since the deaths of Mitotiqui and Francisco I had eaten little. Hearing the cry of a street vendor, he went out to buy a hot tamale, for he knew how well I savoured them.

Our neighbours had known of my liking for Francisco. Even had they not, we could not have hoped to conceal Eve. The only dogs in the city were small and hairless, their barks as high-pitched as a chicken's cluck. Eve declared herself Spanish in every huge bone, every long hair, every booming bark. She marked us as collaborators, and it was my father who paid the price.

Returning from the vendor, the tamale clutched in one hand, he was confronted by a group of brutish warriors.

The rough shouts from the street penetrated my daze. Slowly, for my body was loath to do my bidding, I went to find the cause.

My father was a craftsman, not used to fighting. He was no match for a band of louts armed with cudgels. By the time I reached him he was already down, splayed on the ground, limbs outstretched like a spider. The treat he carried for me had been crushed underfoot. Red chilli mingled with his blood.

I howled in pain and set upon the warriors, my woman's fists beating uselessly on their backs.

"Spanish whore!" they called me. A fist struck my jaw, and my mouth filled with blood.

I would have perished in a storm of blows. But the dog Francisco had called coward leapt to my defence. The warriors' hatred of me was not equal to their terror of Eve. Snapping, snarling, the huge animal was a fearsome sight. She had barely begun to fight when they fled.

My father was not dead. Not yet. But I could see that his wounds were mortal. A deep cut had severed the veins in his neck. His life was spilling onto the street.

No one came to help me. The neighbours who had stood watching slipped silently away into their homes, and I was left to drag my father to his bed alone.

And alone, I watched him die.

I thought I could endure no more. That the gods had laid me as low as it was possible to be. That there could be no greater depths of misery. I wished for death; I longed for it. The endless night of Mictlan could not be bleaker than the city I dwelt in.

But then a sickness came. Spiralling outwards from the palace, it first took those who had lived closest to the Spanish. It raised angry spots on the flesh and brought a raging fever that burned so strong that people plunged into the cold waters of the lake seeking relief. It was so violent that once it had struck, it did not abate until it carried its victim away on flaming wings of death. It swept through Tenochtitlán like fire sweeps across the hills in times of drought. Hundreds ... thousands fell with it.

A quarter, one half, two thirds of the city lay in its clutches. It carried away our emperor, Cuitlahuac; our priesthood; farmers; slaves.

It took Mayatl.

Crops grew untended in the chinampa fields; ripened maize went unpicked. The streets were deserted, and over each house hung a fearful hush pierced only by groans of suffering and cries of mourning.

And yet the sickness did not take me.

For those who die of disease go to the eastern paradise. The gods would not allow me this.

I was condemned to live.

Francisco had said that the human heart is fragile; it must cleave to something. He had spoken true. I had lost my brother, lover, father, nurse. My crippled heart sought an object to cling to before I was driven mad with grief and loneliness. Unthinking, I allowed my feet to carry me towards the peasants' district at the northern limit of Tenochtitlán.

I went to my grandfather's dwelling. A two-roomed hut, it stood on wooden supports on the edge of the lake. It was like an island, cut off from the city by a thin canal. A set of planks made a bridge, giving access to the doorway. Telling Eve to sit and wait, I walked across it, calling as I went.

I had seen little of my relations. On occasion we might pass in the street, or at the marketplace, but that was the limit of our acquaintance. Farmers and craftsmen do not mix. I thought this was the only reason we saw them so rarely. I did not realize how much my father had protected me.

There was no one else I could approach. I did not even know where my father's parents lived. And besides, they had disowned him; they would be unlikely to admit he had a daughter, much less give her aid.

My mother's family, though, was a different matter. Being farmers they could have no unwieldy sense of pride. Though I had seen little of them, I thought they would recognize me – had my father not said I was the image of my mother? But they would have no knowledge of what had lately befallen my father. I would have to explain all.

I had reached only the middle of the plank bridge when an aged woman appeared in the doorway thrusting a sharpened pole before her as if to defend herself. I took her aggressive stance to be simple ignorance of my identity. She was an old woman – perhaps her sight was not as sharp as mine; perhaps she could not make out my features. She gave no greeting, but I thought little of it. I pitied how embarrassed she would feel when she knew I was her daughter's child.

Stretching my hands towards her, palms upper-most in a gesture of supplication, I spoke.

"I am daughter of Yecyotl, and of Oquitchli the goldsmith."

I had expected her mouth to crease into a smile of recognition, but it remained impassive. She made no reply.

"Do you not know me?" I persisted. "Your name is Temolin, is it not? I am Itacate, your grand-daughter."

Still her face showed nothing. Confused, I began to wonder if her hearing was right – perhaps, like her sight, it was impaired with age.

I spoke louder, more clearly. "Alas! My father is dead." I paused. Swallowed. Drew deep breaths. For a few moments, I could not continue. Then, wip-ing the tears that coursed down my cheeks, I said, "I am left alone. I seek your protection."

"Go." She spat the word. It splashed like poison between us.

I blinked. Looked at her face. Her mouth was a thin, hard line. "*Go?*" I echoed, not understanding.

"Go back to your own home," she said harshly. "You are not welcome here. Neither you nor your ill fortune."

"But…" I gasped, "you are my kin!"

"No. We do not choose to own you. You have

no family here. You will not bring the gods' wrath down on our heads too."

"But—"

"You deny it? It was predicted at your birth and the priests were right. The moment you were born you brought disaster. You killed your mother! My daughter! If your father had possessed the sense of an ant, he would have left you upon the mountainside to die. He should have sold you as a slave. None but a fool would have nurtured you. And now he has been punished."

She waved her stick at me as though she could drive me away by force. She had no need to. The sight of her eyes scalding me with hatred and loathing was enough to make me turn on those thin planks and limp wounded away.

At last I saw clearly the gods' intent. At last I could trace the pattern they had drawn at my birth. I was cursed. I had been told it often but had long resisted the truth, nourishing a hope that the predictions would be proved wrong. That I could escape my destiny. How could I have been so foolish?

Had I remained in my allotted place, perhaps only those closest to me would have been stained by my ill fortune, and the damage contained within the walls of our dwelling. But I had not. I had tried to step aside, and all the people of Tenochtitlán had suffered for it. My brother had gone unwillingly to sacrifice in jealousy of me. He had dishonoured the god, and I was to blame. In his great wrath Tezcatlipoca had avenged himself on the whole city. Had I not seen him strike the Spanish leader and thus provoke the massacre that followed? Had he not sent a plague to destroy those who had evaded the Spanish swords? So much blood it had taken to appease him! And I was the cause of all its shedding.

Knowledge of my guilt weighed so hard upon me that my soul was compressed, crushed, until it was hard and black as obsidian. And with that hardness came a new resolve.

I would not sink into despair to please the gods; I would not plunge into the abyss of misery they opened up before me. They had drawn this path, and I was compelled to walk it. But I would not hang my head in shame. Even now, I defied them.

In those dark, cold days Eve was my only comforter; my only protector. Having neither task to occupy my hands, nor companion to speak to, I walked with her. And I walked tall, chin held high, deaf to the whispers muttered behind raised hands, blind to the fingers that pointed accusingly. From sunrise to sunset we tramped relentlessly, mile upon mile, like the shadows of the unburied dead; the restless spirits that haunt the highways; the wandering soul of Francisco.

I did not cross the principal causeway along which the Spanish had fled. Though the burnt bridges that linked the sections of stone had been replaced, too many dead still choked the waters, filling the air with foul vapours. Instead we went out through the market across the causeway closest to my home, and from there into the hills beyond, where Mayatl had once led Mitotiqui and me in search of flowers. With Eve at my side, no one challenged me. Looks there were, certainly – hostile stares and murmurs of contempt. The dog showed me for a Spanish whore: a betrayer of my people, a blot upon the city. A whore, moreover, so little valued that she had been abandoned by our enemy when they left.

I could go where I pleased. Do as I liked. No one ordered me home. No one told me to remain in the valley. I could roam free; cross the mountains and see what lay beyond; walk to the coast and behold the great ocean which had carried Francisco to our land; view the jungle he had spoken of with such rapture. And yet each night I returned to my empty home like a beast to its lair. I did not leave my city. I found I could not. I was tied to it, as though tethered by an invisible thread, which jerked tight if I wandered too far.

❊ ❊ ❊

It was a terrible winter. Every face I passed was pinched with woe. All eyes were dulled with hunger. But when the days began to lengthen, and the chill grip of the season loosened its hold, it seemed possible that some semblance of life might continue.

One morning I was woken early by sunlight streaming through the windows of my empty house. The air was balmy and a gentle breeze blew down from the hillsides, sweetly fragranced with the scent of newly opened flowers. I had walked like a living corpse through the months of winter, but now I felt the freshening spring stir something in me: something akin to hope.

Sensing the energy within me, Eve leapt to her feet, tail wagging, loud bark splitting the still dawn air. It was a summons to walk, and I obeyed, setting forth across the causeway to the hills beyond.

This time I climbed and felt no tug of thread pulling me back. I strode loose-limbed, energetic, delighting in the healing warmth of sunshine on my face.

But the god who had slackened my leash did so for a reason. Cresting the ridge for the first time in my life, I gazed at the vista beyond.

And stopped dead. Air was punched from my chest as though with a sudden blow.

They were far away – perhaps a mile distant.

I could not see their faces. But there could be no doubt as to their identity.

Glinting armour. Iron-shod horses. Men in plumed helmets.

The Spanish had returned.

34

*W*hen I arrived in the market-
place, I found that word had already reached
Tenochtitlán.

A boy ran screaming before me, causing people
to run into the street in alarm. He was stopped in
his headlong flight by a potter whose dwelling was
close to my own.

"What is happening?" he demanded roughly.
"How dare you frighten people thus?"

The boy pointed towards the shore. "The Spanish
are here!"

Panic gripped the crowd. Men cried; women
clutched at their throats.

The potter paid no heed. "Our warriors will drive
them off," he said scornfully. At once the gathered
people murmured in agreement. "Our new emperor,

Cuauhtemoc, will not let them into the city. We shall not make the same mistake twice."

"But there are thousands of them!" the boy protested. "They bring boats!"

"Boats?" exclaimed the potter incredulously. "Impossible!"

"The Tlaxcalans have carried them across the hills. Already they put them to the water! They are coming!"

"The city is impregnable," shouted a different man. "The causeway bridges will be lifted, will they not? They cannot march in. And boats are easy to repel." He laughed at the folly of our enemy.

Another called, "How can they fight from the water? From canoes? It cannot be done! They will tire of this and go home."

But they did not tire, and they did not go home.

Slowly, patiently, their canoes circled the city, gliding calmly, distantly, where our warriors' arrows could not reach. As the darts plopped uselessly into the water, mocking laughter rippled across the lake. Our enemy did not attempt to attack.

I started to see the reason for the many pleasure trips Cortés had taken with Montezuma upon the lake. The Spanish leader had mapped the city well. He knew exactly how to strike with most effect.

He did nothing.

Holding us trapped within our city, he waited.

No traders came from the hills bringing meat to market. Crops ripened in the fields but no one could harvest them, cut off as we were by the Spanish boats. Food could not reach us, either by road or by canoe. And then the pipes that carried sweet water from the mountains were cut.

We began to starve.

Eighty days.

The struggle for Tenochtitlán lasted eighty days.

People said we were deserted by the gods, but I could hear the malicious glee of Tezcatlipoca and I knew it was not so. In the dead of night he stalked the streets. In the long days of siege and battle he ran amok amongst the warriors. Often I felt the chill of his presence, the icy breath in my hair, the cold fingers pressed below my ribs. But when I turned my head to look, he was gone, leaving the sound of his laughter echoing in my ears.

All around me I watched my neighbours, eyes growing big in their gaunt faces, cheeks sinking, skin hanging slack over bone. We ate what we could. Lizards. Reeds from the lake. Deer hide. Leather. Weeds. Dirt.

It was Eve who saved me from starvation. I had

no skill, no knowledge, of how to obtain meat. She hunted at night, and often I dreamt she was crossing the causeways, leaping the gaps, swimming between bridges to reach the shore, and returning to me with slabs of well-cooked meat stolen from the table of a Spanish captain. But in reality she did not leave the city. In the morning she brought what she could find in the streets and presented it to me as though I were her pup: a bird, a rat, a mouse. Not appetizing fare, but enough to keep death at bay.

The Spanish force held our warriors within the city. And when we were sufficiently weakened with hunger, our enemy came across makeshift bridges. With huge guns they battered a toehold for themselves in the southern districts of Tenochtitlán. Daily they came nearer, fighting their way north towards Tlaltelolco.

Every street the Spanish took, each leafy avenue they conquered, was then laid waste so that our warriors could not take to the roofs and hurl rocks down at them. The magnificence of Tenochtitlán was turned into a pyre of flaming buildings, a wilderness of smoking rubble. The bathhouses, the temples – all fell. We knew they had reached the palace when the cries of burning birds were carried on the wind, and singed feathers and blackened fur blew about the ruined streets. Screaming roars of panthers pierced the sky. For they had put torches to the emperor's aviaries. The menagerie.

The air was noxious with the sulphurous reek of gunpowder and the stench of bodies. The dead lay unclaimed, unburied, rotting in the open air.

Francisco had once told me of a goat that lived in his land: a creature with fearsome horns. In the springtime, when the fresh grass sends forth its shoots, the males fight, rearing up on their hind legs and ramming their skulls together with such force that the sound of their blows echoes across the valleys. Sometimes their horns become entangled and the beasts cannot pull apart no matter how hard they struggle. Locked together, they lose their footing and plunge into the crevasse, smashing down onto the rocks below.

Our leaders were locked in such a battle. Neither would yield; neither would surrender. And the prize each fought to win – the splendid city of art and flowers – was daily dashed into smaller and smaller fragments and rendered worthless.

Driven before the Spanish came refugees from the south of the city. A slow trickle at first: those who sought sanctuary with relatives, friends. But soon the trickle became a stream, and then a raging torrent which flooded into Tlaltelolco until the district seemed to drown in people. Old men bloodied and beaten, dying of their wounds. Women and children wide-eyed with shock, arms and legs as brittle as sticks, bellies swollen with desperate hunger, too shocked to whimper or cry at their distress. Too weary to speak at all. My home was mine no longer, but the last refuge of any who had survived thus far. Ours was the last stone building of the district. Beyond lay only peasants' huts, chinampa fields, the lake, Spanish boats.

No one could look upon the faces of these people and not burn with anger. It was rage that drove Cuauhtemoc. Fury. And the more hopeless the fight, the stronger burned the hatred. Not only in him but in us all.

They reached the edge of Tlaltelolco on the eightieth day. And when our emperor called for wives to take up their fallen husbands' weapons and fight our enemy, they went forth, hearts full of courage, looking small and foolish in their borrowed armour.

I found Mitotiqui's cudgel. Thus armed, I went into the street to fight.

I had no knowledge of killing. In times past I could not even wring the neck of a chicken – such tasks had always been Mayatl's. If I could not take a bird's life, I doubted I could take a man's. Yet neither could I sit and quake in a corner. I was possessed of a wild, reckless courage, for I knew I could not die. Those gloriously slain in battle entered paradise. The gods would not allow me that honour. When I set forth, I knew I was invincible.

The familiar road before me was empty. But from beyond the houses of my neighbours came the sounds of battle. Yells of warriors. Screams of women. Gunfire. Smoke.

Mouth parched, palms wet with sweat, I strode towards it. I had pulled most of my skirt between my legs, and tucked the cloth into my waistband to fashion a pair of makeshift breeches. I would not be impeded by my clothes. Eve was beside me, her trotting gait transformed into a reluctant slink, ears low, mouth frothing anxiously.

I came to the corner, rounded it, and my warrior's career almost came to an end. A horse reared above me, iron hooves thrashing through the air by my head. There was no time to think. Grasping it with both hands, I swung Mitotiqui's cudgel, shutting my eyes as I did so, expecting those hooves to strike me at any moment.

A terrified whinny. A loud clatter. Spanish screams.

I opened my eyes and saw my blow had struck. The horse was down, flailing upon the stones, its belly ripped wide open, insides spilling, bloody and hot, on the street. Its weight held the rider pinned to the ground and his face was contorted in agony.

I had no pity. The sorrow and rage of all I had suffered and seen flared from me, and with a great cry I swung once more. Felt the obsidian bite. Heard his gasp. Saw the gaping wound and knew the man was dead. Startled by my success, fearful of the thrashing hooves and bellows of the dying horse, I fled.

Running, I made for the market, where the noise of the fiercest fighting seemed to be. I came swiftly round the corner, where a narrow alley ran beside the canal, to find my path blocked. A bloodied Spaniard, sword raised, stood before me. With a yell I held my cudgel aloft, but his sword was already above me. I dodged, though I knew I could not avoid the blow.

But Eve was barking. A loud, joyful sound. A greeting.

And I saw the clay fragment about his neck. The imprint of my lips.

"Francisco?"

The Spaniard twisted. The sword sliced past my face and fell clattering onto the stones.

For a moment, we stared, too shocked to move. And then, with a cry of rapture, I was locked in his fierce embrace. We clung together so hard that we could not get any closer, and yet still it was not enough. I dug my fingers into his flesh, for I could scarce believe that he was real. He was solid! Warm, vibrant – not the lost spirit I had mourned. A sob tore from my throat. Hot tears spilt from my eyes and ran into his golden hair. Francisco pressed fervent kisses on my neck, my face, and I laughed aloud in joy. He was alive! How was it possible?

Drawing my head back, I took a long, starved look at Francisco.

I would not have known him. His face – once perfect as Tezcatlipoca's – was scarred and distorted by the blow that had severed his ear. His once-smooth skin was pockmarked by the sickness that had killed so many in my city. And his eyes, which had once blazed with laughter and life, were now dulled by horror and despair. Seeing me dressed as a fighter he wept, the tears running down his cheeks.

Wiping them away tenderly, I whispered, "I thought you were dead!"

He pulled me against him, and his breath was soft and warm in my hair. "Knocked senseless ... but not dead."

"But Eve came to me..."

He laughed, and the sound was dry and cracked with lack of use. "She ran from the battle. Did I not tell you she was a coward?"

I did not say how she had saved me. For as we

stood, arms wrapped tightly about each other, an eerie quiet descended on the city.

Our emperor was slain. I knew it. The strange calm could mean nothing else. Cuauhtemoc was gone. The battle was lost. The empire was no more.

But still I lived.

As did Francisco.

We listened to the sounds of warriors throwing down their weapons. The taut hush was strung out like a thread and then snapped by a Spanish yell. A triumphant shout. And then came the swell of their chatter. Laughter. Excitement. Relief. And above it all, Cortés's dreadful cry.

"We have victory! Now we shall find where they have hidden the gold."

Francisco seized my hand. "We must get away from here," he said urgently. "God alone knows what our soldiers will do now they are victorious."

I laughed. A strange, high sound that rang with hysteria. "Where, Francisco? Where are we to go? You think there is anywhere in this city we can hide?"

"There must be somewhere, Itacate. Think! Believe me, you do not want to be found."

His eyes begged, pleaded with me to provide an answer; to offer a place of safety. He grasped my hand, tugging it as my brother had once done.

With that small gesture came the reply.

"There is somewhere," I answered, and I saw the faintest flicker of hope ignite in his deadened eyes. "How well can you swim?"

Slipping into the murky canal that ran beside us and swimming slowly northwards, we moved in the direction of the chinampa fields. What was left of the streets was now full of my people fleeing the city. For as soon as the battle was over, the Spanish had begun to loot it.

The water was putrid, choked with the remains of the dead, and it was a repellant task to swim through it. But only here did we have a chance of moving unobserved. Eve kept to the land, following us like a grey shadow, passing unremarked amidst the chaos and ruination.

When soldiers ran by, we had to plunge our faces into that poisoned water and float, corpse-like, hoping that not even a Spaniard would loot a drowned body. When we reached the main canal, we moved so slowly that to an observing eye it would look as though our lifeless forms were carried by a current. Before us was the causeway. We drifted towards it.

Much effort it took us not to cry out at the sight before us. A bridge had been laid, and starved, gaunt women with their bony-faced, round-bellied children made a slow, limping procession across it towards the distant shore. A group of soldiers stood clustered at the far side. Before anyone was allowed to pass, they were searched, lest they carried gold upon them. Children's mouths were yanked open, women's skirts ripped apart. In view of all, rough Spanish fingers probed their most private places.

Stiff with rage we passed beneath the bridge and edged onwards. Here sharpened poles had been thrust into the bed of the lake as defence against the Spanish boats. With care we squeezed between them, but we could not avoid cutting our flesh and tearing what few clothes remained on our persons.

Reaching the chinampa fields undetected, we lay pressed close together in the decaying vegetation where once I had played with Mitotiqui. I could feel my brother's presence. See the ghost of his infant self spinning. Calling. Laughing.

When night came, we moved once more. We dared not cross to the nearest shore: it was too full of Spanish soldiers and their Tlaxcalan allies. With the aid of a broken canoe we aimed to swim across the lake to the eastern shore and escape over the distant mountains.

It was nigh impossible. I knew it even as we began.

We swam, clinging to the upturned vessel with

Eve between us. There was no moon and the sky was so cloudy that not even a star was reflected in that black water. It seemed to stretch infinitely before us – we were crossing a drowned world. We dared not speak, but forced ourselves onwards while I shivered with both cold and terror. I feared we would be spun into Pantitlan, or that Tlaloc would seize me by the ankles and drag me down to the lake bed.

Yet he did not. After a long time the canoe bumped against the land. So weary that we knew not where we were or how close was the Spanish force, we dragged ourselves onto the grass.

"And now?" I asked Francisco.

"We wait for sunrise."

Sunrise?

How could it come? With no priests to let their blood, no hearts burning on altars to nourish the god? This night would not cease. It could not. Perpetual darkness would now reign. Mictlan was come to earth. The fifth age was ended. We would perish.

Eve whined. I said nothing to Francisco, but he too felt my fear. He gathered me to him and held me tight.

"It will come," he promised. "Dawn will come. Be sure of it." But his own voice trembled with doubt. This was not his land. His god had no power here.

It was long past the hour of the dawn, of that I was

certain, and yet still the sky was dense and black.

But then I felt the weight of it lessen. Perceived the slightest lightening of its gloom. I blinked. Once. Twice. Rubbed my eyes lest it prove to be a cruel trick played by the gods.

But no. In the distance was a line of grey. As I watched, it broadened. And as I stared, my teeth began to chatter. I started to shake uncontrollably.

"Do not be afraid," Francisco murmured.

When the first ray of sunshine pierced the horizon, I shook still. I could not cease. Yet it was not with fear, but with bitter fury. And with burning excitement.

The sun was rising. No priest drew his own blood to make it happen. No living heart was plucked to feed it. No conch blast called forth the dawn.

Yet it came.

They were wrong. Priests. Wise men. Soothsayers. Emperors. They had always been wrong. So many people had been slaughtered for a false belief! So many had climbed the temple steps to gain life everlasting.

Paradise. Mictlan. Both melted away like mist as the sun climbed higher. It warmed my flesh and my heart beat faster. The blood thrilled in my veins.

For if the priests had been so wrong in their teachings, then perhaps they had been wrong about me too. Disaster had come to my city but I was not its cause. I was not ill fated. I was not cursed. The chains slipped from me and in that one radiant moment I knew myself free.

I stood, dazzled, light-headed with joy. "Let us go."

"Where?" Francisco was aghast. "Not to my people?"

"No. And not to mine. We will go to your forest. Your paradise. Your Eden. There we will live."

"In the jungle? Like beasts?"

I smiled. "Like beasts. Yes. With no priests. No gods. We answer for ourselves alone. You and I, Francisco – together we shall make a new world."

Historical Note

The book is based on the history of sixteenth-century Mexico, but while the broad sweep of events is accurate, I've taken liberties in order to make the plot work, altering the sequence of some incidents, ignoring others, and relocating one or two things from Peru and the Caribbean to Tenochtitlán.

While Montezuma and Cortés both existed, I've been fairly free in my depictions of them. In actual fact, Cortés wasn't in Tenochtitlán at the time of the spring festival massacre – his deputy, Alvarado, was responsible for that. To serve the story I have fused these two Spaniards into one character.

Itacate and her family, Francisco and the golden madonna are all inventions; but the dog, Eve, is based on a real hound who was found in the jungle by one of Cortés's men.

Although this isn't necessarily a historically precise book it evokes how it might have felt to live at that time, in that society, with those beliefs, and experience world-changing events at first hand.

T.L.

Bibliography

Primary Sources

Baquedano, Elizabeth: *Aztec* (Dorling Kindersely Eyewitness Guides, 2006)

de Fuentes, Patricia: *The Conquistadors* (University of Oklahoma Press, 1993)

Leon-Portilla, Miguel: *The Broken Spears* (Beacon Press, 1992)

Phillips, Charles: *The Aztec and Maya World* (Lorenz Books, Anness Publishing, 2005)

Phillips, Charles: *The Mythology of the Aztec and Maya* (Southwater, Anness Publishing, 2006)

Salariya, David: *How Would You Survive as an Aztec?* (Watts Books, 1994)

Thomas, Hugh: *The Conquest of Mexico* (Pimlico, 2004)

Wood, Michael: *Conquistadors* (BBC, 2003)

Additional Sources

Bezanilla, Clara: *Aztec and Maya Gods and Goddesses* (The British Museum Press, 2006)

de las Casas, Bartolome: *A Short Account of the Destruction of the Indies* (Penguin, 1992)

Diaz, Bernal: *The Conquest of New Spain* (Penguin, 1963)

Prescott, W.H.: *History of the Conquest of Mexico* (Phoenix Press, 2002)

I was in my fourteenth summer when the Mexicans rode against us. Twelve moons later, I took my revenge. And though Ussen has drawn visions of a terrible future in my mind, I will not be vanquished. I belong to this land: to the wide sky above my head, to the sweet grass beneath my feet. Here must I die.

But first I will live, and I will fight. For I am a warrior. I am Apache.

"Magnificent … a disturbing but exhilarating experience." *The Independent*

"This novel is a masterpiece… It deserves to become a modern children's classic." *Books for Keeps*

"Truly remarkable… It's like Cormac McCarthy for kids – brilliant." *Venue*

BY TANYA LANDMAN

When her grandfather dies, Tamar inherits a box containing a series of clues and coded messages. Out of the past, another Tamar emerges, a man involved in the terrifying world of resistance fighters in Nazi-occupied Holland half a century earlier. His story is one of passionate love, jealousy and tragedy set against the daily fear and casual horror of the Second World War. Unravelling it will transform the younger Tamar's life.

"As fine a piece of storytelling as you are likely to read this year." *The Guardian*

"A fascinating and complex story... Beautifully crafted, with a finale that took my breath away, this is simply unforgettable." *Publishing News*

An advert in the Calcutta Gazette is looking for an apprentice draughtsman to accompany a scholar on an expedition to record avian life in Bengal. How can Anila Tandy, left to fend for herself in a city of rogues, dare to apply for a position that is clearly not meant for her? But the talented "Bird Girl of Calcutta" has never shrunk from a challenge. And perhaps this voyage up the Ganges might be just the thing to equip Anila in her search for her father, missing for years and presumed dead.

Menace and mystery lie in wait for the young girl who sets out to test herself in the man's world of the late 1700s.

"I loved this beautiful story set in eighteenth-century India, with all its sights, sounds and smells." *Jamila Gavin*

"Every page flows with a grace of language unusual in a debut novelist." *The Guardian*

BY MARY FINN